Hello Do You Still Know Me?

LAURIE B. ARNOLD

PROSPECTA PRESS

Published by Prospecta Press, an imprint of Easton Studio Press
P.O. Box 3131
Westport, CT 06880
(203) 571-0781

www.prospectapress.com

Front cover design by Lizzie Sivitz
Cover images © TyBy, © lolya, © BigRyan, © ilusto, © SoRad
Text design by Barbara Aronica-Buck

First Edition

Manufactured in the United States of America

Paperback ISBN: 978-1-63226-061-1
eBook ISBN: 978-1-63226-062-8

To my sons, Jordan and Dylan,
who have shown me the meaning of true magic.

CHAPTER ONE
Surf's Up!

I paddled my surfboard hard past the churning whitecaps as Leroy yowled on the beach. My dog went bonkers when I surfed. Maybe he was worried something bad would happen, but I'd been riding the waves every day since early June when I arrived here in Costa Rica. All I'd ever gotten was one nasty cut on my foot from a piece of spiky orange coral.

"Ride that one! It's perfect!" my best friend Violet shouted from the shore.

"Not perfect enough!" I yelled back as I let the wave roll by.

My friend Noah crouched on the hot-cinnamon sand. His messy brown hair flopped over his freckled forehead as he held Leroy back by his collar. Whenever I surfed, my dog had a habit of plunging into the ocean in his noble attempts to "save" me.

Leroy and I were spending the summer in Jacó, Costa Rica, with Rosalie Claire and her husband, Thomas. Most afternoons, Thomas took a break from his work at the inn and taught me to surf.

Violet and Noah had arrived late yesterday in San José. Rosalie Claire and I drove an hour and a half through the electric-green countryside along a narrow, twisty highway to pick them up at the airport. My friends were joining me for the last two weeks of my summer vacation. It can be tricky mixing friends from different parts of your life, but so far they were getting along great. And number one on their to-do lists? Learning to surf.

I wasn't exactly an expert myself, but most of the time I could make it to shore without wiping out. If only the perfect wave would show up so I wouldn't look like a total dork. I cupped my hand around my firebird necklace, hoping it would bring me luck, and let the wimpy waves pass by.

Violet sprung to her feet. "You can do it, Madison! Holy schnikies, go for it already!" Violet always had the craziest expressions.

When a four-foot wave finally surged behind me, I counted one-Mississippi, two-Mississippi, three-Mississippi. I popped onto my feet and spread my arms, imagining I was a red-winged firebird. Then I shot to shore under a cloudless blue sky.

Surfing is the closest thing I've ever felt to flying.

"Yes!" Violet lifted her fist in victory.

"Awesome!" shouted Noah, giving me two thumbs up.

Leroy barked his applause and wriggled free to bombard my salty legs with soft dog licks.

I peeled off the Velcro surf leash tethering my ankle to the board. Leroy hopped on, standing as still and regal as the Statue of Liberty.

"Move it, Leroy. I have next dibs." Violet motioned to him to skedaddle off the surfboard.

Leroy stayed put.

"Looks like he's trying to protect you, Violet," Noah said. "Maybe he's worried you'll get hurt."

"I can take care of myself, thank you very much. Besides, I've been looking forward to doing this all summer." Violet nudged Leroy's butt. He slinked off, his tail tucked between his legs.

Noah and I watched from the beach while Violet paddled beyond the waves. I stroked Leroy's wiry white fur until he wriggled away to snuffle for crabs in the sand.

Noah had just turned thirteen—a year older than me. I'd met him last summer when we were both contestants on the reality TV show *Stranded in the Amazon*. Since then his voice had turned scratchy as sandpaper. We'd video chatted all year from his new house in Denver where he lived with his dad. When he stepped off the plane, I nearly gasped. He'd grown almost five inches.

"Pretty decent for her first day," he said as we watched Violet teeter onto her knees, wobble to her feet, and then hold her stance for a few seconds before pitching into the surf.

Better than I did my first time.

"Good one!" I shouted. "Now try it without resting on your knees. Just pop straight onto your feet!"

Violet gave me the A-OK sign and kept at it until the shadows from the palm trees edging the beach grew long, and the sun sank low in the sky.

"Sorry. Looks like you'll have to wait until tomorrow," I told Noah. When Violet got super excited about something, sometimes she could forget to take turns.

He shrugged. "No worries. After all, we have two whole weeks."

At least that's what we thought at the time.

After Violet dragged herself from the water, she dropped the surfboard onto the sand and toweled off her long blond hair. It instantly sprang back into a zillion corkscrew curls. It was exactly the kind of hair my grandmother, Florida, wished I had, but didn't. Mine was nut brown and stick-straight, just like my mom's used to be. I liked it that way.

Leroy abandoned his crab hunt and jumped onto the surfboard again, repeating his Statue of Liberty imitation.

"That's it for the day, boy. Come on."

I patted my leg and Leroy followed us up the beach. We wound our way through a thicket of towering palm trees filled with songbirds and chattering white-faced capuchin monkeys. On the other side of the trees was La Posada Encantada, the five-room waterfront inn and café that Rosalie Claire and Thomas owned. Ever since I'd arrived, I'd been staying with them in their saffron-yellow bungalow on the far edge of the hotel.

The whole year, I'd counted the days until I'd be reunited with Rosalie Claire. Until she married Thomas last year, she'd been my next-door neighbor in Truth or Consequences, New Mexico. That's where I live with my sometimes-crazy grandmother, Florida Brown, who I'd moved in with after my mom died. At the time I thought my life was officially over, but thanks to Rosalie Claire, a mysterious TV—not to mention a little magic—my grandmother and I had learned to cut each other some slack. Until recently, that is, when Florida fell back on her old nagging ways. If only my mom could magically appear and tell her to cut it out.

Even though she'd been gone a year and a half, I still found myself thinking about my mom at least every other minute of every single day. Each night before I fell asleep, I double-wished I could see her just one more time. Whenever I had a spare moment, I drew pictures of her in my sketchbook, trying to cement all of the memories I had of her in my brain.

"You're such a lucky duck," Violet said as we walked the winding stone pathway through the inn's tropical garden, blooming with orchids and passionflowers. "You got to be here the whole dang summer!" She picked a purple orchid and tucked it behind her ear.

Given what's happened to me in my life, I didn't exactly feel a hundred percent lucky, but staying here for three whole months qualified as being pretty darn cool.

"I really needed a break from Florida," I admitted. "She started bugging me again about so much stuff, like wanting me to wear make-up and curl my hair. Ugh. I think her biggest dream in life is for me to be Miss Teenage America."

"You're only twelve," Noah pointed out.

"Tell that to my grandmother." When Florida put her mind to something, her will was stronger than a Category Five hurricane. You'd better give in or get out of her way.

"Like you said, sometimes your grandmother can be the absolute worst." Violet gave one of her eye-rolls.

Violet and I had been best friends forever. Since the first day of first grade on Bainbridge Island in Washington State. That's where I used to live with my mom. Violet is the only friend I wanted to be with after my mom died because everyone else suddenly started treating me like I was a different kid. From the minute we met, we'd told each other practically everything, except of course for the stuff that might hurt her feelings. But I knew for a fact I'd never told her that Florida was the *worst*. I'd only said she'd been super crabby. Way more than usual. And that I'd hoped it was just a temporary setback.

"It's on account of my teensy headaches," my grandmother would say after she'd scream at me or send me to my room for something tiny, like accidentally letting Leroy track dust into the house. Then she'd lie down on her bed with the curtains drawn shut.

I worried maybe something was wrong because until her headaches started, Florida had tried to be a better grandmother. She came to at least half of my afterschool soccer games, and for the longest time she'd laid off trying to turn me into a girly-girl. Which, for the record, would be about as easy as getting my dog to sprout wings and fly to Jupiter. I made her promise she'd go to the doctor while I was gone. I figured she must have been getting better because during our Sunday morning phone calls, she sounded as if she was almost back to her old self.

Violet, Noah, Leroy, and I wound our way past the tiki bar next to the hotel swimming pool. A man in a swimsuit and a woman wrapped in a flowery sarong shared a chaise lounge. They gazed at each other all lovey-dovey as they sipped a drink through two bendy straws stuck in the hole of a coconut shell.

"Newlyweds," I whispered. "Hope they last longer than the couple that stayed here in July. They got married on the beach at sunset, then kept everyone up all night, fighting. The next morning they asked Rosalie Claire to recommend a good divorce lawyer."

"Sounds like Florida and your Grandpa Jack," Violet said.

True. Except my grandparents never officially divorced. They just lived in two different places and saved their fighting for when they were together.

As we climbed the steps to the whitewashed verandah outside the lobby, we noticed a foul odor drifting through the door.

"Wow. Smells like the boys' gym," Noah said.

"Or something dead." Violet scrunched her nose.

"Or both," I said.

Here's one thing I've learned about living in a hotel: you never knew who or what you'd to bump into. One whiff and my nose told me exactly who was inside.

CHAPTER TWO
The Unexpected Guest

Surfers. I recognized the no-deodorant rotten compost smell I've come to know and not love in Jacó. La Posada Encantada was a favorite with the surfers since it's right smack on the beach. Two guys in their twenties stood in front of the desk. A stringy scraggly-haired one and the other shaved bald as a soccer ball.

Usually Sofia, the front desk clerk, checked in guests, but today was her day off. Rosalie Claire was behind the counter, her fingers flying on the ancient computer keyboard. Her coffee-colored skin was shiny with sweat from the Costa Rican heat and her braided black hair was partly covered with a red bandana.

"Dude, you've got like, a dinosaur computer from the Ice Age. Does it run on electricity or does it eat meat?" The scraggly-haired guy snorted at his own joke.

"A new computer's on our list." Rosalie Claire's sparkly brown eyes crinkled with a grin. "You must be Riptide Atkins. Welcome."

"That's me. In the flesh."

"The gross and smelly flesh," Violet whispered.

Rosalie Claire handed Riptide a key to Room Five.

"Dude, we need two. One for me and one for Wingnut." He motioned to his buddy.

She unzipped the battered tan leather fanny pack she always wore around her waist, fished inside, and pulled out another key.

"Cool." Riptide stuffed it in his pocket.

But he had no idea just how cool Rosalie Claire's fanny pack really was. It was magic. She kept regular things in there like anybody would, although if she needed something to help somebody out, then *presto*, it would just show up.

"Madison, would you kids kindly show Mr. Atkins and his friend to their room?" Rosalie Claire smiled her secret smile, as if she knew exactly what I was thinking about their stinky armpits.

The two surfer guys grabbed their surfboards and their bags, and followed us outside down the open breezeway. We passed Room Two where a pile of fresh white folded sheets sat by the door.

"Lady in White's staying there. She's terrified of dirt, only wears white, and changes her own sheets three times a day. She won't let us touch them," I whispered to my friends.

"Looney tunes." Violet made the "crazy" sign, her finger twirling circles beside her ear.

"Pretty much. We sometimes have the strangest guests checking in. OK, here we are. Room Five."

"Thanks, dudes." Riptide unlocked the door. As soon as he opened it, Wingnut left his surfboard outside and lugged in his suitcase.

Riptide patted his shoulder bag. "Well, gotta go chill and play me some Battle Wizards."

"Awesome game." Noah gave Riptide the thumbs up.

"You know it, dude." Riptide leaned his board next to Wingnut's and dragged his duffle through the door.

We headed back down the breezeway toward the lobby. A pile of trays with dirty dishes now sat in front of Room Three.

"The old guy in there must have just put them out," I whispered. "He says he's a travel writer. He showed up the day after I did and nobody's seen him leave his room since."

"How can anyone write about travel if they never go outside?" Noah wondered.

"My thoughts exactly. Unless he's writing a book about room service."

Violet, Noah, and I carried the trays back to Thomas's Café. Leroy trotted behind us, probably hoping the leftovers would miraculously fly to the floor.

The inn's kitchen was a beehive of busyness with Thomas bustling alongside his employees, Miguel, Arturo, and Rose, as they prepared for the dinner crowd. His white apron looked like a painting I might have done in preschool. It was splattered with black from beans, red from salsa, and bits of something green. Thomas always whistled while he cooked, either theme songs from cartoons or the tunes from his childhood in the Dominican Republic. That's where he'd lived until he moved to New Orleans with his family when he was ten. Today it was the theme song from *Scooby Doo*.

When Thomas noticed us with the trays, his licorice black eyes lit up.

"You kids are hired! How'd you like to stay here all year and help out? I'll pay you in compliments and all the food you can eat," he joked.

"Will. Work. For. Food." Violet's eyes shone at the thought.

I giggled. "She'd do it. She's a bottomless pit!" More than once I'd watched Violet eat an entire large pepperoni pizza. All by herself. Never *ever* does she gain a single ounce.

And me? I would have *loved* to stay all year, but soon I'd be going back to Truth or Consequences. Only two weeks left of my summer vacation before I'd be reunited with my cranky grandmother.

"There you are!" Rosalie Claire scurried into the kitchen. "Since you three have been on the beach all afternoon, you must be starving. What do you say we spoil your appetites with a backwards dinner? Dessert first?"

"Yes, please," I said, because I knew what was in store.

We pulled up stools at a narrow wooden table in the corner of the big industrial kitchen, its chrome counters polished to a shine. Rosalie

Claire served us three fat slices of her famous blueberry pie. Then she unzipped her fanny pack and pulled out a jumbo Milk Bone for Leroy. He sniffed it and hung his head.

"Tired of Milk Bones? Who can blame you, boy? They *are* a little on the dry side."

Leroy thumped his tail in agreement.

She dropped the Milk Bone into the trash and poked around in her pack. Out came a gigantic juicy bone.

"Try this," she said, and Leroy snatched it.

"Holy guacamole!" Violet's eyes went wide. "That thing is *huge!*"

"How'd you do that? How did it even fit?" Noah stared at the fanny pack.

Rosalie Claire smiled. "A magician never reveals her secrets."

"But how does it work *scientifically?*" Noah asked.

Rosalie Claire shrugged. "Honestly? I'd tell you if I knew, but I don't. There actually might be a good scientific explanation, although I've always chocked it up to one of life's great mysteries."

"Speaking of magic, this blueberry pie is almost as magical as your fanny pack." Rosalie Claire may have spoiled Leroy with meaty bones, but she spoiled me with her pie. It tasted exactly like my mom's. Kind of like summer sunshine sprinkled with sugar. That's because when my mom was a kid, they'd both learned from the pie master herself, Rosalie Claire's Grandma Daisy.

Grandma Daisy had lived next door to my mom when she was growing up in Truth or Consequences. She would go over there as much as she could. My grandmother *hated* that. Partly, I think, it was because Grandma Daisy was African-American, just like Rosalie Claire, and Florida was as white as vanilla pudding. I think my grandmother was prejudiced, although she'd never admit it. And the other part? My mom liked hanging out with Grandma Daisy a whole lot more than she did with her own mother.

By the time we finished our pie, the sky had turned into an orange sherbet sunset.

"How is it possible that my stomach's growling like a garbage disposal? We still get dinner, right?" Violet asked.

"Of course. Otherwise it wouldn't be a *backwards* dinner," Rosalie Claire said.

After we'd eaten plates of rice, black beans, and fresh snapper caught that day in the sea, we headed to the yellow bungalow. Violet and I shared the double bed in the guest room and Noah flopped down on a futon on the floor.

"*Could* you stay here the whole year instead of going back to New Mexico?" Noah asked as he pulled up his covers. "You'd be able to surf every day after school."

The thought made my heart feel as warm as the noonday sun.

"Admit it, Madison. It would be awesome. Then I could visit you during every single school vacation." Violet yawned, tired from all the time she'd spent in the ocean.

I agreed it would be *super* awesome. From the second I arrived at La Posada Encantada, I'd felt as light as air. I couldn't remember feeling that way since before my mom died.

Leroy sailed onto the bed, sandwiched between Violet and me, and promptly fell asleep. The three of us yawned in unison, listening to the crashing waves on the shore, the *whoosh-whoosh-whoosh* of the ceiling fan, and the *rat-a-tat-tat* of Leroy's snores keeping the beat like a snare drum. Finally, we nodded off, first Violet, then Noah, then me.

I don't know how long I'd been asleep, or even if I'd dreamed, when a wild racket jolted me awake.

Someone was yelling my name.

I crept out of bed and peered through the window into the moonlit night.

Outside in the stone courtyard stood my grandmother, Florida

Brown. She lugged a suitcase large enough to fit half the contents of a department store.

Before I could answer, she collapsed onto the ground in a dead faint.

CHAPTER THREE
Florida Comes to Stay

By the time Rosalie Claire and I got my grandmother into the bed in Room Four, she'd come to and didn't remember fainting.

"My goodness, let's not make a fuss. It's only a tiny touch of exhaustion, probably because getting here was an utter nightmare. I made a teensy mistake and accidentally told the taxi driver to take me to the wrong town three hours in the opposite direction." Florida yawned and her eyelids grew heavy. "Oh my, this bed feels divine."

"Are you sure you're all right?" Rosalie Claire's eyebrows knit together with worry.

"Did you faint because of your headaches?" I asked.

"I'm perfectly fine." Florida's voice sounded thin and tired. "I just wanted to see you, Madison." She clutched my hand and drifted to sleep.

I went back to my room and slipped quietly into bed so I wouldn't wake Violet. It was a surprise and a comfort to know my grandmother had missed me. I tried falling back asleep, but Leroy's snores, the crashing of the waves, and my worries about Florida kept me up until the sky turned light on the horizon.

I didn't wake up until ten o'clock, after dreaming about Florida fainting in every imaginable place. She'd fallen off building rooftops, from craggy cliffs, and even into a giant bathtub full of green Jell-O.

Violet, Noah, Rosalie Claire, and I went to Thomas's Café for a late breakfast of icy watermelon juice and *gallo pinto*, a combination of rice, black beans, onions, peppers, and salsa with tortillas. We were eating on the patio beneath the shade of the feathery palm trees when Florida sashayed in, movie star-style. She was back to her old glamorous self. Every dyed red hair had been teased and sprayed into place. Her ruby lipstick was drawn on in a perfect pout. The second she spotted us she lit up. I almost kicked myself for losing sleep worrying about her half the night. She looked as if she felt better than ever.

"Well isn't this the most adorable place! I already feel like a new person. Must be the salty sea breeze. It will be just the thing to keep my complexion moisturized."

She slipped into the wicker chair beside me.

"Oh, that coffee smells heavenly! Honey, could you pour Florida a nice full cup?"

For the record, I wasn't allowed to call my grandmother anything other than Florida because the word "grandma" made her feel old.

As I was about to pour her coffee, Thomas swooped in with a fresh pot, his eyes twinkling as he bowed.

"Our V.I.P. guest deserves only the best. Fresh coffee hot off the press for our visiting royalty. And Madam, you certainly don't look old enough to be anyone's grandmother."

"Well, aren't you the most divinely observant man?" Florida gushed.

Thomas winked at Rosalie Claire before returning to the kitchen. I'm pretty sure she'd given him the heads up that he'd have an easier time with Florida if he buttered her up with compliments.

Florida sipped her coffee, chattering about her favorite beauty products, the nosy new neighbors who'd bought Rosalie Claire's old house next door, and how her best friend Patsy had gotten fat.

Nobody could get a word in up, down, or sideways.

Finally, Rosalie Claire cupped her hand on top of Florida's. "It's wonderful you've come all this way to see Madison. How long will you be staying?"

"Oh, not long." Her mouth pressed into a hard red line. "Actually, I have no idea." Then she stared off at the Pacific Ocean.

"Is something else going on, Florida?" Rosalie Claire looked at her with those warm brown sugar eyes that made even the most hardcore liar want to take the witness stand and tell the whole truth and nothing but the truth.

My grandmother twisted her napkin.

"Is Jack OK?" Rosalie Claire wondered.

"Jack? Oh, he's fine." The flatness in her voice made it sound as if she didn't mean it.

"Is something wrong with Grandpa Jack?" My grandfather lived a couple of hours away from Truth or Consequences, although he was never far from his phone. He kept me sane whenever Florida went off the edge. If something was wrong with him, I wouldn't know what to do.

"No, he's *fine*." She exhaled a sad sigh. "The day after you left for summer vacation, he moved back in with me as an experiment. But after two-and-a-half months I deserve an angel's halo for putting up with Mr. Can't-Do-Anything-Right. I'm sure he's thrilled that I'm gone."

Florida drained her coffee, stuffed her balled-up napkin in the empty cup, and forced a smile.

"We're all going to have ourselves a barrel of fun, aren't we, honey? In fact, this place is so charming, maybe I'll stay with you and your adorable little friends for the rest of your vacation!"

Violet rolled her eyes and kicked my shin under the table.

Noah shot me a look, waiting to see what I'd do.

And me? I sat there, in a state of shock. My grandmother had just crashed my summer vacation. I felt like jumping onto my surfboard and riding it far away across the sea.

ı

CHAPTER FOUR
Call the Doctor!

We abandoned our surfing plan because Florida insisted that we show her the sights of Jacó. I could tell my friends were super disappointed, but they didn't say a word, they were just quieter than usual. We'd only made it four blocks when my grandmother got all wobbly in the knees and turned as pale as eggshells.

"On second thought, maybe I need to sit down for a minute." She sank to the curb and rubbed her forehead.

"Did you ever go to the doctor?" I asked.

"This'll go away. It always does," she said, waving away my question. "Honey, I need some Tylenol."

"I'll go find some," Violet said, and Noah volunteered to go with her. We weren't far from the Best Western. I gave them the 3,000 *colones* I found in my pocket, and they took off down the wide palm tree-lined driveway toward the resort's gift shop.

Florida and I waited under the hot midday sun. Even though I felt like yelling at her for not going to the doctor, I couldn't. Number one? I never yell. And number two? One look at her and I knew she felt as sick as a dog.

Violet and Noah returned with the Tylenol and a bottle of water. I offered her two pills. She insisted on three.

"We should just go back to the inn. Can you walk OK?" I asked.

"What do you think?" Florida snapped. "Do I look like I can walk?" She moaned and dropped her head into her hands.

See what I mean about those headaches making her crabby? Whenever she was nasty like that I wanted to hide, but I knew she needed help.

It was Noah who came to the rescue. "I've been running cross-country all year. I'm on it." He took off like a shot back to La Posada Encantada.

He was super fast because not more than fifteen minutes later, he and Thomas pulled up in the red pick-up. They helped my grandmother into the front seat. Noah hopped in the back of the truck with Violet and me.

"She'll be OK," he said.

I hoped Noah could predict the future.

Back at the inn, we led Florida into the lobby. Sofia was behind the desk, so Rosalie Claire devoted her full attention to my grandmother. Her eyebrows scrunched up with worry. "Florida, you're still ill, aren't you?"

"I wish you would all stop your fussing. It's just a case of the come-and-go flu. I've had it on and off for months. I'll be better soon." She slumped onto the sofa. "My goodness, could somebody turn down the air conditioning? What are you people doing? Trying to turn this place into the North Pole?"

The North Pole? Even with the fans spinning full blast, it had to be at least eighty degrees in the lobby.

Rosalie Claire felt my grandmother's forehead and took her pulse. She told her she suspected this was no flu.

While Violet, Noah, and Leroy hung out by the swimming pool, Rosalie Claire and I led Florida back to Room Four. She fell into bed and I covered her with blankets.

Rosalie Claire unzipped her fanny pack, but all she found was a cool wet washcloth and her cell phone that she always kept in there. "How odd," she said under her breath. She shrugged and spread the cold cloth on Florida's forehead.

Whenever someone was sick, Rosalie Claire's fanny pack usually delivered vials of tinctures and small pouches of healing herbs. Was a wet washcloth all Florida needed to get better?

My grandmother pulled the covers over her head and groaned.

"I'm calling the doctor," Rosalie Claire whispered to me.

An hour later, when Dr. Morán knocked on Florida's door, I let him in. His bushy dark beard and chubby cheeks made him look like a short, round Santa whose hair hadn't yet turned white. He carried a beat-up black leather bag stuffed with supplies. I hoped something in there would contain a cure.

I went back to the lobby and hung out with my friends and Leroy while Rosalie Claire stayed with Florida and the doctor. It seemed as if he was in there forever. When we finally heard the *click-click-click* of his leather shoes on the tile floor, my breath caught in my throat. I jumped up from the sofa and felt the pounding of my heart.

"What's wrong with her?" I asked.

"I suspect it's malaria. She has most of the symptoms. Rosalie Claire told me that you and your grandma were in the Amazon jungle last summer."

I nodded.

"Sometimes malaria doesn't show up for a while," Dr. Morán told us. "All it takes is one bite from an infected mosquito."

On *Stranded in the Amazon*, zillions of bugs had chomped on us like we were a five-star gourmet buffet. When we got back to Truth or Consequences, we'd both taken medicine so we wouldn't get the disease, and that's what I told Dr. Morán.

"If you forget to take all the pills, the symptoms can show up months later," he told me.

I took all my medicine. Had Florida stopped taking hers?

"Will she be OK?" My voice was barely a whisper, probably because I was afraid of his answer.

"The pills I gave her should kill the parasites. I would expect her to improve a little each day."

By early the next morning, Florida was worse. We awoke to her shouts bouncing through the lobby, across the courtyard, and through our open bedroom window in the yellow bungalow.

The three of us scooted in our pajamas toward her room, with Leroy trotting at our heels. The newlywed lovebirds, the Lady in White, and the two surfer guys had already gathered in the breezeway, watching Rosalie Claire as she tried the locked door.

"Florida, please let me in!" She jammed the master key into the lock, but she didn't even have time to turn it.

The door burst wide open. My grandmother charged out like a thundering bull chased by its worst nightmare.

"I'm under attack! Giant tarantulas! Move it, people!"

What was going on?

We scurried out of her way so we wouldn't get bowled over. Leroy barked from all the excitement.

Florida took one look at Leroy and her eyes nearly popped from her head.

"Ack! A man-eating T-Rex!" She made a beeline for the lobby.

Leroy took after her, playing a rowdy chasing game.

Rosalie Claire bolted after them both.

"Dude, that lady has some gnarly imagination! Totally radical!" Riptide high-fived Wingnut like this was some kind of circus show.

"That lady is my grandmother and she's super sick."

"Oh, man. Sorry to hear that, dude." At least he sounded as if he meant it.

By the time my friends and I got to the lobby, Rosalie Claire had corralled Florida. They sat on the sofa, Rosalie Claire's arm draped around my grandmother's shoulders. Leroy had stopped impersonating a T-Rex and was stretched out peacefully on the white tile floor.

When she saw me, Florida's eyes opened wide. "Angela, honey. What are *you* doing here?"

Whoa. How weird was that? Now I *knew* something was super-wrong with her. Angela was my mom and if she'd still been alive she would have been thirty-four years old. I was twelve.

"She must be hallucinating," Rosalie Claire whispered. "I'm wondering if those pills didn't agree with her."

Noah asked to see them. They were teeny-tiny, half-blue, and half-red. He got on the lobby computer and did a Google search. Apparently those pills could be bad news.

"It says here the medicine can also cause bizarre behavior, confusion, hallucinations, and mood changes. Particularly if someone is mentally unstable to begin with."

Unstable? That's practically my grandmother's middle name.

Just then, Florida began scratching her skin as if fire ants were gobbling her alive. Seconds later she erupted from head to toe in an explosion of itchy red spots.

"Oh, and hives. That's another side effect," Noah added.

Florida sprung to her feet and raced half-crazy around the lobby. When she passed a mirror hanging on the wall, she stopped and stared. Then the screeching started. "It's a red-speckled monster! Everybody run! Alien invasion!"

Violet and I exchanged looks as Florida raced in circles around the room. We wanted to laugh but stopped ourselves. It might have been funny if my grandmother hadn't been so sick.

Rosalie Claire unzipped her fanny pack. This time she found cotton balls and a bottle of pink calamine lotion. "Madison, you put this on your grandmother's spots while I call Dr. Morán. This may be more serious than we thought."

She guided Florida back to the sofa. As I dabbed her skin with the cool pink liquid, she squirmed from the itchiness. Her breathing turned soft and shallow. My grandmother was gasping for air.

"Dr. Morán wants to run some tests," Rosalie Claire said when she got off the phone. "He cancelled his next appointment. He's rushing right over."

The doctor must have thought it was serious too. Could my grandmother die?

CHAPTER FIVE
The Magic Fanny Pack

When Dr. Morán came out of Room Four, we were all waiting. Violet, Noah, Rosalie Claire, and me. He said he'd taken blood from Florida's arm and made her pee in a cup. He was going to have it all tested to double-check that she had malaria. He was especially worried because the whites of her eyes had turned a sickly scrambled egg yellow.

"The results should be in by early evening," he said. "The hallucinations could mean she had a bad reaction to the medication. You'll need to watch her closely for the next few days until it's out of her system. Unfortunately, the color of her eyes would suggest that she's getting sicker." Then he hurried back to the clinic.

Rosalie Claire decided it was best to move Florida into my bedroom in the bungalow so she could keep an eye on her. My friends and I hauled our stuff to Room Four, where we'd sleep until my grandmother got better.

Violet, Noah, and I went back to the bungalow while Rosalie Claire got some work done around the inn. That way we could listen for my grandmother, in case she needed something. We found a deck of cards in the living room and played Crazy Eights on top of the old leather trunk that doubled as a coffee table. Ever since Rosalie Claire told me the trunk had once belonged to her Grandma Daisy, something about it gave me the shivers. It was as if it connected me to the past and Grandma Daisy, who was magical just like Rosalie Claire.

Leroy stood guard at the bedroom door. Florida slept the rest of the afternoon, waking only once in a panic to report that twelve microscopic blue men were camping out in her jar of wrinkle cream.

Late that night, my friends and I were still in the bungalow with Rosalie Claire and Thomas when the doctor finally called.

"It's not malaria," Rosalie Claire said when she hung up the phone. She closed her eyes and breathed deep. When I asked her what it was, she said the doctor didn't know. "He thinks it could be some rare disease she picked up in the Amazon jungle. He's never seen anything like it. He's asked some tropical disease specialists to help him figure it out. We may not know for a few days. Maybe more. If your grandmother gets any worse, they want to airlift her to the hospital in San José."

The hospital?! I *hate* hospitals. The last time I was in one was when my mom died. That was the *last* place I wanted Florida to go.

I remember my mom used to say that things happen for a reason, except I couldn't see any reason for so many people in my life to leave me behind. My dad disappeared when I was a baby. My mom died. Was it possible that my grandmother could leave me too? My eyes stung hot with tears.

Rosalie Claire pulled me close.

"Does the doctor think she could die?" I whispered.

"He won't know anything until they figure out what's going on." Her eyes were damp as she stroked my shoulder.

I laid my head on Rosalie Claire's lap and my tears splashed down my cheek, spilling onto her fanny pack.

Her fanny pack! It *had* to have exactly what my grandmother needed to get better.

"Madison, what do you say we use a little magic?" It was as if Rosalie Claire had read my mind.

I bolted upright, drying my eyes on the back of my hand.

"This time let's go for something more powerful than a wet

washcloth, cotton balls, and a bottle of Calamine lotion." She slid open the zipper of her pouch.

"Once again, my Rosalie Claire is about to save the day." Thomas beamed at her from across the room.

But when she reached into her fanny pack, all she pulled out was her cell phone.

Her face froze in shock. "What in the world?"

"Maybe it's too much to ask of your pack. Curing a rare jungle disease is a tall order," Thomas said.

"It shouldn't matter." Rosalie Claire looked as confused as I felt.

"How could it just stop working?" Violet asked.

Rosalie Claire sighed. "It *has* been acting up lately. For what it's worth, I do remember Grandma Daisy saying that everything expires after time. Bodies, milk, even magic. It's lasted well over thirty years without needing a recharge, but now is a rotten time for it to quit working."

"The magic can be *recharged?*" asked Noah.

Rosalie Claire nodded.

"Then let's do it! What are we waiting for?" Could it be that Florida's cure was right around the corner?

Rosalie Claire didn't look as excited as I did.

"If only it were that easy. As far as I know, it can only be recharged with a rare piece of Baltic amber that belonged to Grandma Daisy."

Grandma Daisy had been dead for nearly five years. What had she done with that stone?

A familiar feeling rushed over me like a gust of warm wind. I stared at Grandma Daisy's old leather trunk. The one that gives me the shivers. With a sweep of my hand, our playing cards flew to the floor. There was something in there that we needed. I just *knew* it. I *felt* it. My gut told me that maybe, just maybe, it was the magic piece of amber.

CHAPTER SIX
Treasures in the Trunk

I unlatched the rusty clasp and pushed open the lid, its hinges creaking from old age.

Rosalie Claire let out a heavy sigh. "I looked through it when it first arrived. I can't say I remember seeing the amber, although maybe I missed it."

We gathered around the trunk and peered inside. It was jam-packed with ancient treasures. We discovered raggedy yellowing books on herbal remedies, shape shifting, and black magic. Thomas and Rosalie Claire gathered up all the ones on herbs and began to read, hoping to find a cure for Florida's mysterious disease.

My friends and I kept digging.

Violet found Grandma Daisy's dusty red leather-bound photo album. The edges of the black construction paper pages were tattered and torn.

We thumbed through the fragile black-and-white photos. Mostly they were pictures of fifteen-year-old Rosalie Claire, taken the summer she came to live with Grandma Daisy in Truth or Consequences, right after her parents died. Instead of the braids she now wore encircling her head, they were wild and loose, like an explosion of twisty snakes.

"Nice hairdo." Violet giggled.

"My Medusa period." Rosalie Claire smiled at the memory. "Not my best look."

Thomas disagreed and said he thought Rosalie Claire looked as pretty as a rosebud.

I'd read about Medusa in my book of Greek mythology. Her hair had been turned into a mass of wriggling snakes after she got in trouble for marrying Poseidon, the God of the Sea. She spent the rest of her life being generally nasty and turning people into stone. The total opposite of Rosalie Claire.

"Madison! Check it out! You were such a cute baby!"

Huh?

Noah waved a greeting card in the air. "Your baby announcement!"

I snatched it from his hand and stared at the photo. My mom and dad beamed from the picture as they held me up to the camera. Written at the bottom were the words:

ANGELA BROWN AND DANNY MCGEE
ARE THRILLED TO INTRODUCE THEIR NEW DAUGHTER,
MADISON.

My mom must have sent it to Grandma Daisy after I was born.

"I've never seen a picture of my dad before." I couldn't take my eyes off the photo. It was a revelation. Mostly I resembled my mom with my stick-straight brown hair and pale freckled skin, but I saw that I had my dad's broad nose and his bright blue eyes.

"What happened to him, anyway?" Noah asked.

"No idea. My mom always said she thought he died, although nobody knows for sure. He just disappeared. Right, Rosalie Claire?"

"I'm afraid so." She sighed and her mouth pinched tight.

"He left when Madison was a baby," said Violet, who knew me better than almost anyone.

"Kind of like my mom, except I was seven when she took off," Noah said. "She sent an e-mail to my dad saying she'd moved to Chicago."

I wondered what it would be like to get a note from my dad saying he'd been living in Chicago all along. Weird.

I could have stared at that photo all night, but we had work to do. We plowed through the rest of the stuff in the trunk. Not far from the bottom we found a heavy cardboard box. We set it on the floor and lifted the lid. Dozens of crystals and colorful rocks glistened under the lamplight.

"This could be it." Violet's eyes gleamed as bright as the crystals.

One by one, we picked out the stones and examined them until we came across a chunk of amber. It looked like a nugget of hardened golden honey.

"Score!" Violet lifted it up in victory.

"Oh my, let's see!" Rosalie Claire set down the remedies book and Violet handed her the amber.

"Is it the magic piece?" I asked, realizing that in the blink of an eye my grandmother could be back to normal again.

Rosalie Claire sighed. "Sorry, it's not. The one we need has a tiny frog trapped inside. In fact, my grandmother was never quite sure if it was the frog that was magic or the amber. I always thought it was the combination."

"Wait a minute," said Noah. "Since amber was liquid tree sap that hardened, couldn't we just melt that piece down, press a dead frog into it, and let it harden again?"

Rosalie Claire shook her head. "If only that would work, Noah. Sadly, there's no tricking magic."

"And where in the heck would we find a magic frog anyway?" Violet asked.

Violet was right. There were about a bazillion gift shops in Jacó and I was pretty sure not one of them carried ancient dead magic frogs.

We were just about to give up hope when we found an old videotape at the bottom of the trunk. On it was a tattered sticker. "Daisy's Special Remedies," it said, handwritten in black Sharpie. I felt a tingly rush of hope.

"Maybe Grandma Daisy says something about curing rare jungle diseases." I handed the tape to Rosalie Claire. Was *this* the thing my gut told me I needed to find?

"This could be the answer to our prayers." Rosalie Claire kissed the black plastic case. "Now where's our old tape player?"

Thomas retrieved it from the top shelf in the hall closet and hooked it up to the TV in the corner of the living room.

The image on the tape was scratchy from age. Even so, I could still make out the famous Grandma Daisy. I'd always imagined her being surrounded by silver sparkles of fairy dust, but when I saw her in action, I could tell that the sparkles lived right in her eyes, the same way they did in Rosalie Claire's. My mom used to say you could tell a lot about a person just by looking into their eyes. She said it was a window to their soul. Grandma Daisy's soul must have been filled with a galaxy's worth of glittery magic.

On the tape, she sat at her kitchen table in the house next door to where my grandmother and I still lived in Truth or Consequences. It looked almost the same as when Rosalie Claire had lived there except for one big difference. Thumbtacked on the wall was a calendar, flipped to May 1994. The tape had been recorded nearly twenty years ago.

For an hour Grandma Daisy talked about remedies. She recommended herbs for fighting the flu, for curing stomach cramps, and getting rid of warts. She suggested magical crystals to treat headaches. She didn't mention a single word about rare tropical diseases.

By the end of the tape, my heart felt as if it had been hit with a hammer. I'd been so sure that this was what I was supposed to find. Rosalie Claire must have sensed how I felt. She wrapped her arms around me and we touched forehead-to-forehead.

"We'll think of something," she whispered. "Don't give up hope, Madison. I can feel in my bones that the universe will deliver something. I just don't know what it is yet."

I wished I felt as sure as she sounded.

Even though it wasn't even eight thirty, we were all dog-tired. We told Rosalie Claire we were heading to bed. "Why don't you kids get some fresh air and take the long way around through the garden? Being outside usually makes things better."

I slipped my birth announcement into my pocket. Then I peeked in on Florida. She was muttering something in her sleep about accidentally buying a vicious warthog from a shopping show when she'd meant to order a diamond ring.

"We'll figure something out," I whispered, even though I knew she couldn't hear me. "I promise."

I headed outside into the night with Violet, Noah, and Leroy. A gigantic full moon lit up the garden. Rosalie Claire had been right. It felt good to be outside. It was still warm enough to be in shorts, but a slight breeze cooled my skin. We followed the trail behind the inn, being careful to whisper so we wouldn't wake the guests as we passed their rooms. Only Riptide and Wingnut's light was still on. We could hear the beeping sounds of computer games through their open window.

My brain buzzed a million miles a minute. Why hadn't we found anything in that trunk when my gut said we would? Did we miss something in the videotape that contained the secret we needed?

I glanced up at the night sky just as a billowy cloud slid across the moon. Clouds always made me think about my mom. It may sound weird, but there's part of her that lives up there in those clouds. When things get tough I talk to her and I'm pretty sure she's listening. I concentrated hard, trying to remember the sound of her voice. A gust of wind swirled around my legs and I almost felt as if she were with me. I spoke to her in my head because I didn't want my friends to think I was crazy. *Mom, I lost you,* I thought. *I can't lose Florida, too. Tell me what to do, OK?* If only she'd appear by my side and guide me. I watched for a sign as the cloud danced in front of the moonlight.

That's when it hit me. Maybe the video *was* the answer. Maybe, if we got the MegaPix 6000 back, I could teleport into it while the tape was playing, the same way I had into a real TV show. Then I could zap with Rosalie Claire's fanny pack to the past and ask Grandma Daisy to recharge it.

And if I went into the past, would I get to see my mom?

I watched as the cloud evaporated into the night sky.

CHAPTER SEVEN
Miracle Movers

We settled into our room. Noah laid down on his futon on the floor. I crawled into bed, and after Violet switched off the lamp, she sailed in next to me. She could barely contain herself. "So what you're saying is, if we had the magic TV, we could travel to the past? How awesome would that be?"

"That's what I'm thinking. Except I don't even know if it works with a videotape. Or how we'd get the TV back."

"Can you track down the guy who delivered it the first time?" Noah asked.

"Mike? I have no clue where he is. Or even where he came from."

We whispered in the dark until I heard my friends' soft breathing and Leroy's snores. I tried to sleep, but a slew of thoughts ping-ponged through my head. I kept thinking about Florida, my mom, and my baby announcement. I switched on the reading light and stared at the photo. At last I had proof in a picture that my dad had looked happy to be my dad.

I dug out my drawing book and got to work. I loved to draw. Sometimes I did it to entertain myself. Other times it helped me to make sense of things, and that's what I did tonight. I sketched my family, hoping it would be a small way to reunite the three of us in pencil and etch the image into my memory.

I was adding the final shading to my drawing when I heard a curious screech. Leroy barked and leaped off the bed.

"Lee-roy, shush," groaned Violet.

"Yeah, go back to sleep, buddy," Noah yawned.

Leroy whined.

A funny feeling came over me. A tickle in my gut that I couldn't ignore.

"Guys, I'll be right back. I need to check something out," I whispered.

"I'm up now. Might as well come with you." Violet slipped on her flip-flops.

"Me too." Noah rubbed his eyes.

The three of us tiptoed down the breezeway in our PJs, into the darkened lobby. Two headlight beams sliced through the front window, lighting up the room like a soccer field at night.

When I opened the front door you could have knocked me over with a tropical breeze. The Miracle Movers delivery truck, dents and all, was parked outside. Mike got out, checked his clipboard, and scratched his scruffy red beard.

"Hello, Squirt! Your MegaPix 6000 has arrived!" Then he winked.

The magic TV was back!

Had my mom heard me ask for the MegaPix? It wasn't the only time she'd helped Mike deliver a little magic. Last summer after he'd picked up the TV from our house in Truth or Consequences, he told me he could sense what my mom wanted by reading her messages in the clouds. OK, maybe that sounds a little bit eerie, but it was definitely awesome.

"Hey, can you kids give me a hand?" Mike asked. "I'm traveling solo tonight."

The three of us helped him haul the enormous flat screen MegaPix 6000 into the lobby of La Posada Encantada. Violet volunteered to get the videotape player.

"Not so fast, Short Stuff. It won't do you a bit of good," Mike told Violet. "We've got a slight hitch. The last fellow who used this gadget teleported himself from New York City into a National Geographic documentary. He had a close encounter with a lion who mistook the remote control for dinner. Swallowed it whole. Now the poor man is stuck in Africa, maybe forever."

Last year, when I'd first told Rosalie Claire about the MegaPix, she'd warned me about the dangers of magic. At the time, I couldn't imagine what could possibly be so risky, but after nearly dying in the Amazon and now hearing about this guy stuck in Africa, I understood.

"So the bottom line, Squirt? We're down to zero remotes."

OK, here's the thing. I was kind of responsible for the first missing remote control. When I'd zapped into *Stranded in the Amazon*, the TV host took it from me. He'd stuffed it into the pocket of his safari jacket. Then he'd hung it on a tree branch. I'd tried to retrieve it, although I wasn't fast enough. A spider monkey got to the jacket first and hurled it, remote control and all, into the Amazon River.

Without a remote control, the MegaPix 6000 was useless.

"So, here's the deal. Before you can help your grandma, you're going to have to find that remote you left back in the rainforest."

OK, magic or no magic, it was still a little weird that he knew my grandmother needed help.

"It's probably at the bottom of the river. Or in the belly of some crocodile," I said. How in the world would we find it?

"Wait a minute. If you're magic, can't you just, you know, *poof* us another one?" Violet pretended to wave an invisible magic wand through the air.

Mike stared at her as if she'd asked him if gravity was something he'd just made up. "It doesn't work that way. First of all, wands are only in fairy tales. And second of all, you can't just magic *everything* out of thin air. It took a lot of engineering along with a little magic to make those remote controls. Oh, speaking of magical engineering, I did bring along this handy-dandy gizmo."

He presented us with a shiny black high-tech gadget, about the size of a cellphone.

"The GammaRay Particle Scanner. GPS for short. Use this baby to track down the remote. If it's around, the GPS will find it. Even if it's stuck in the guts of a crocodile."

Oh boy, I hoped we weren't destined for a spine-chilling round of crocodile wrestling.

"But it was lost in *Brazil*," said Noah. "Which is approximately 2,000 miles from here. How do we get there?"

"You kids'll figure it out. I have confidence in you." Mike winked again.

"Has anyone ever used a videotape with the MegaPix to zap back in time?" I asked.

"Not so far, although there's a first time for everything. Sign here, Madison. Then I'll be on my way."

He handed me two copies of the contract. They looked like the ones Florida had signed without reading when Mike had delivered the TV to us in Truth or Consequences. I made sure to read every single word.

"Basically, it means we have to be super careful and the MegaPix people aren't responsible for anything, right?"

"It's always good to read the fine print." Mike grinned.

I signed my name on the dotted line beside the big black "X". One copy I handed to Mike, and the other I kept for myself.

"Well campers, safe travels!" With a wink and a salute, Mike headed out to his rattletrap truck.

Violet, Noah, and I ran outside to watch the Miracle Movers truck bounce down the potholed road. Just as it had back home, the truck screeched, backfired, and then shimmered in the night. We watched as it dissolved into wavy lines, finally disappearing into thin air.

Violet bounced with excitement. "Holy guacamole, that was seriously cool!"

"Not to mention a screaming fast way to commute from New York City. Or wherever the heck he came from. How does he *do* that, anyway?" Noah ran his fingers through his floppy brown hair.

As much as I would have liked to know the same thing, we didn't have a spare second to think about it. We had something more important to figure out. How to get ourselves back to the Amazon Rainforest.

CHAPTER EIGHT
Riptide to the Rescue

Back in the lobby, we hovered around the GPS, staring at it as if any second it would reveal its great secret. Even Leroy sniffed it, trying to uncover its mysteries.

Finally, Noah flipped it over. He slid open the back and found a slot for a USB cable connector. "I think I know what to do." He took the device over to the lobby computer but couldn't find a USB port to plug it in. The computer was too old.

"Holy schnikies, they need to order a new computer, and fast," Violet said.

"That could take weeks," I pointed out. I wasn't sure Florida had that much time.

"I've got it!" Noah's eyes shined brighter than a cake full of candles.

Somehow I knew exactly what he was about to say.

"Riptide and Wingnut. Come on, let's go."

With Noah in the lead and Leroy picking up the rear, we raced down the corridor to Room Five. A ribbon of light streamed through the bottom edge of the surfers' door. I knocked. Riptide opened it, peeking out through squinty eyes. Then he broke into a broad grin.

"Dudes! Like I totally wasn't expecting you! Are we having a pajama party or something?"

"Not exactly. We need to use your computer, if that's OK." I vowed not to say a word about the MegaPix. It was best to keep the secret to ourselves.

"Yeah, we need to plug this little gizmo into your laptop." Violet pointed to the GammaRay Particle Scanner in Noah's hand.

Riptide stared at it. "Whoa. What *is* that thing?"

"It's sort of like a virtual detective game," Noah said. I was glad he covered for me since I'm a lousy liar.

"Sounds totally epic," Riptide said.

The room looked as if the guys had packed explosives in their suitcases and when they'd opened them, their clothes erupted everywhere. We picked our way over the piles to the desk by the window.

Leroy leaped onto the bed, making himself at home on a wad of wet board shorts next to Wingnut. Wingnut was glued to his computer, wearing headphones over his shaved head as he listened to the *kabooms* and *kapows* of videogame warfare.

Riptide paused his game of Battle Wizards and Noah connected the mysterious device to the laptop. The GPS whirred to life. In a flash, the screen turned pitch black.

"Oh man, did that thing just crash my computer? I was about to capture a three-headed dragon and level up."

"I hate it when that happens," Noah said.

Just when we thought we'd have to restart the computer, a bright blue text box popped on the screen.

"Looks like it's time for you to sign in." Noah nudged me. I scooted my chair over to the keyboard.

Here goes nothing, I thought. Or *something*, I hoped.

I typed in my name and made up a secret password. Then some text popped on the screen:

Hello, Madison! We've been waiting for you!

Who had been waiting? How did they know? I kept reading.

Congratulations! You are now the proud owner of the Gam-maRay Particle Scanner™. Your GPS will detect gamma rays embedded in the MegaPix 6000's remote control.

Our mapping system can pinpoint the location of the gamma ray device within a three-mile radius.

Once the GPS is within that radius, it will beep and a red light will flash. Beeps and flashes will become more rapid as the device moves closer to the remote control.

"Wow! A high-tech game of warmer-cooler!" Violet scooched in closer to get a better look at the screen.

Noah could barely stand still. "So *that's* how the MegaPix works!" Uh-oh.

"Wait. Whoa. What's a MegaPix?" Riptide looked confused.

Violet covered quickly. "Um, it's just part of this whole game."

"It's like a magical teleporter," Noah added. "A *pretend* magical tele-porter."

"Gotcha," Riptide said.

Noah took a deep breath, relieved that his mess-up hadn't spilled our secrets.

"So how *does* it work? In the uh, *game*, I mean." I was itching to hear what Noah had figured out.

"OK, here's what I *think* happens. The gamma rays in the remote must break matter down into pure invisible energy so things can tele-port. Then once the energy is out of the gamma ray force field, it assem-bles back into solid matter."

"Whoa! Matter, dude?"

"You know, like *people*. People are matter. Chairs are matter. Dogs are matter. We're all matter. Anything solid is matter."

"Well, I'm totally solid, man, and I matter." Riptide chuckled at his own joke. "Sounds like an awesome game. So are you some kinda super brain?"

"Not really. I just read a lot of stuff."

But I was realizing more and more that my friend Noah was officially a brainiac. Not to mention modest.

Next I clicked on a tiny map that grew to fill the screen. It was dotted with twinkly gold lights that quickly dissolved and left behind two flashing red targets. One was in Kenya on the continent of Africa. That's where the remote-control eating lion was probably experiencing a massive case of indigestion. The other was about 2,000 miles southeast of Costa Rica.

"Brazil!" I said.

"Not far from where we did *Stranded in the Amazon*," Noah whispered to me so Riptide couldn't hear.

I shrugged. I didn't have any idea exactly where we'd been in Brazil since Florida and I hadn't arrived by airplane like everyone else. We'd traveled there by magic, through the MegaPix.

"How do we get there?" Violet asked.

"Maybe it's like Battle Wizards. You look for clues in the game," Riptide suggested.

"That's one idea," I said. "Personally, I think we should ask Rosalie Claire."

"Whoa. You mean the lady at the front desk? She's a *video gamer*? Sure wouldn't have guessed that!" Riptide looked impressed.

"Life sometimes has a way of surprising you," I said.

It was getting late. I clicked on *quit*. Another text box popped up on the screen:

Are you sure you want to quit? Do you need transportation?

We gawked at the message. It was as if somebody knew exactly what we needed.

"Click 'yes!'" Violet got so excited that she reached over and clicked the computer mouse for me.

A cool graphic of a high-tech airplane zoomed across the screen, pulling behind it a banner with this message:

Our luxurious supersonic Astral plane will meet you tomorrow morning at the Quepos Airport—10:00 a.m., sharp. Don't be late.

Tomorrow morning? It was almost midnight. We didn't have much time to pack.

We thanked Riptide, who laughed and waggled his head like a springy bobble head. "You know, this game of yours seems gnarly cool. It would be totally awesome if you showed up at the airport and that plane was waiting for you. Like for real."

Little did he know that's exactly what we were counting on.

For the first time since we'd arrived, Wingnut glanced up from his computer game. "Hey, when did you guys get here?" His eyebrows scrunched into a unibrow.

Leroy leaned over and licked Wingnut's whiskery chin.

"Chill out, dude. You got yourself some gross dog breath."

"Maybe because the dude is a dog," Violet said.

We thanked Riptide, hurried to our room, and packed our back-packs. I threw in some snacks, just in case. Then we headed for the yellow bungalow to find Rosalie Claire.

CHAPTER NINE
Rosalie Claire

We only made it as far as the lobby. Rosalie Claire, wearing her tattered honey-colored robe, stood in front of the MegaPix 6000, staring.

"*Mike* was here?" Her wide eyes grew even wider.

Wait a minute! *Rosalie Claire knew Mike?* My face must have looked so confused that she answered my question before I could even ask it.

"I've known Mike for years, back when Grandma Daisy owned the Wildflower Mercantile."

Wildflower Mercantile was the dusty old shop in downtown Truth or Consequences that sold crystals and herbs. It was famous for its magical remedies.

"How did he know where to find us?" I figured if Rosalie Claire knew Mike that well, maybe she'd also know how he had a knack for showing up at exactly the right time.

"That, Madison, is one of Mike's many mysteries."

I wondered what other mysteries Mike kept locked up in his vault of secrets.

"I must admit, I never thought I'd be happy to see this crazy TV contraption again. Although I think we can put it to good use this time, don't you, Madison?" Then she smiled. I had a feeling Rosalie Claire knew exactly what I planned to do with that videotape.

"Yep," I said. "Unfortunately there's a slight glitch."

We told her about the missing remote, the GPS gizmo, and our plan.

"So we'll need a ride to the airport first thing in the morning," I told her. "OK?"

"Not OK."

Uh-oh. Rosalie Claire hardly ever said no.

"Look, I trust you kids, except I can't let you go by yourselves to Brazil. Not on my watch."

"But . . ."

"But nothing. I'm coming with you."

And you know what? I was relieved.

"Who's going to take care of Florida?" I asked.

By then Thomas had wandered in sleepy-eyed from the bungalow.

"Sir Thomas at your service," he yawned. "I just hope Florida doesn't start hallucinating again. Herding giant spiders and dinosaurs is not my finest talent."

Rosalie Claire threw her arms around his neck. "You, Sir Thomas, are my knight in shining armor. And that's no hallucination."

"Flattery will get you everywhere." He planted a kiss on her head, next to the topknot of her curly black hair.

Early the next morning, I tiptoed in to see Florida. She twisted and turned. Her face was as red as a poppy and her forehead felt like it was on fire.

I kissed her cheek, something I'd never done before because Florida wasn't the kissy type.

"I'll hurry as fast as I can," I promised. And then I ran off to join Rosalie Claire and my friends who were waiting for me in the car.

CHAPTER TEN
Astral Airlines

The bumpy road to the airport snaked along the endless blue Pacific Ocean. Rosalie Claire did her best to dodge the zillions of potholes. I sat in the passenger seat, gazing up through the windshield at the cotton ball clouds that seemed to follow our car as we sped south. I imagined my mom up there, keeping an eye on me, and I thought about Leroy, who'd whimpered when we'd left him behind with Thomas.

"What happens if we find the remote but the MegaPix doesn't let us go into the past?" asked Violet.

"It *has* to work," I said, because it was the only thing I could think of that might help save Florida.

An hour later when we pulled up to the airport, Violet gasped. "Whoa! Are we traveling on a flying chicken? The place looks like a barn."

That's exactly what it looked like, except it was the color of mustard. The teeny open-air shack sat in a bright green field in the middle of nowhere. The place didn't even have a front door.

"We better hurry, it's five minutes to ten." Noah bolted from the car.

The four of us sprinted across the dirt parking lot and into the airport with our backpacks. Inside was a chalkboard, posting the day's departures.

"Uh, guys? There's no listing for Astral Airlines." Noah looked worried.

"Never heard of it," the man behind the check-in desk told us when we asked.

Oh great. Was this the beginning of a wild goose chase?

"I think we should wait anyway," Rosalie Claire said.

We sat on white plastic chairs at the back of the building where we had a perfect view of the landing strip. When a small propjet touched down on the runway, we got our hopes up, but it was only delivering sacks of mail. It was already 10:45. Our plane was missing in action.

"It's not coming," sighed Violet.

"Oh, I think it is," Rosalie Claire assured her.

All of a sudden I felt it too.

At eleven o'clock we heard a piercing whine, even though the sky was empty except for the puffy cotton clouds. A tiny rickety gunmetal-gray plane appeared from out of nowhere. Its engines groaned as it touched down on the hot gray asphalt. It bounced and roared to a stop, not far from where we sat. I could barely make out the faded blue words painted on the side: Astral Airlines.

"They call that hunk of junk *luxurious*?" Violet snickered.

"Looks more like a bucket of bolts," I said.

The airplane door creaked open.

"Your chariot has arrived. Sorry I'm late, Squirt."

Mike?! Seriously?

Mike, looking official in a navy blue pilot's uniform, poked his head through the door.

"Well look who's here," Rosalie Claire said with a twinkle in her eye. "You could have at least knocked on my door last night and said hello."

"It was late. I didn't want to bother you. Besides, I had a feeling I'd be seeing you soon." Mike winked at her and motioned us toward the plane. "Come on kids, time to get crackin'!" He slid out a metal ladder that screeched and hit the pavement with a clang.

I scrambled up first, wondering if this dilapidated beast could make it all the way to Brazil without going down in flames.

When I got inside, I could hardly believe my eyes.

CHAPTER ELEVEN
The Flying Deathtrap

The plane may have looked tiny on the outside, but inside it was *gigantic*. It reminded me of a super ritzy living room. A limousine-sized leather sofa lined one side, and along the other wall stretched a glass dining table for eight. At the back of the jet stood a regulation-sized pool table, which is a pretty weird thing to find on an airplane.

"OK, *this* is what I call cool!" Violet dropped her backpack onto the paisley rose-colored carpet.

"Now I'm a little less worried about getting us to the Amazon," Rosalie Claire admitted. "That's assuming you really know how to fly this thing, Mike. You *can* fly a plane, right?"

"I got it here in one piece, didn't I? Besides, they say a chimpanzee could fly this thing. So sit back, strap yourselves in, and let's ride this baby into the skies!"

The four of us sank into the sofa. It was so squishy soft it nearly swallowed us whole. On the coffee table sat baskets of foil-wrapped chocolates and sugar-sprinkled gummy worms.

I liked this plane more and more every minute.

The second we clicked on our seatbelts, Mike pushed the throttle and we barreled down the runway.

Our takeoff was whisper quiet as the Astral plane lifted us into the air.

"Open the tabletop and grab yourself some breakfast," Mike called back to us.

"Hope there's lunch too. By my calculations it's going to take about five hours," Noah said as he tilted up the top of the coffee table. Inside we found little boxes of cereal, steaming hot fried egg sandwiches, fruit, and ice-cold containers of milk.

I chose a box of Froot Loops. As I ate my breakfast, I kept thinking about what might lie ahead in the Amazon jungle. The last time I was there I nearly died plunging over a waterfall. How could it get any worse than that?

We tried playing pool. Violet neatly broke the triangle of balls. They wacked around until the plane dipped and every single one of them skittered to the left side of the table, dropping straight into the pockets.

"Sorry about that. They're still working on steadying this thing." Mike shrugged.

Out the window the clouds shot by faster and faster.

"Woo-hoo!" he yelled. "Just hit Mach-1! Seven hundred and sixty-five miles an hour."

"That means we broke the sound barrier! All right!" Noah raised his fist in the air. "It sure won't take five hours at this speed!"

"Brainiac," Violet and I said at exactly the same time, and then we giggled.

We were traveling so crazy-fast I figured there was no question that we'd make it there before lunch.

Since the pool table was useless, we strapped ourselves back into our seats on the sofa and found a deck of cards in the coffee table drawer. We'd just slapped down a round of Crazy Eights when Mike unbuckled his seat belt.

"Bathroom break. Don't worry, the plane's on autopilot." He made his way back to the restroom.

Rosalie Claire had just won the first hand with an eight of hearts when a robot voice blared from the cockpit's computer.

"System overload. System overload."

We heard Mike's muffled yells through the closed bathroom door. "What'd it say?"

"System overload," Rosalie Claire shouted back. "That can't be good."

The computer boomed out its warning again. *System overload. System overload.*

We heard the toilet flush, followed by a sharp rattle. The bathroom door was shaking.

"It's locked!" Mike banged on the handle.

Rosalie Claire was about to unclip her seatbelt to go help him when the cards flew across the table and fell to the ceiling. Chocolates and gummy worms sailed through the air.

The plane had spun upside down.

We screamed and clutched the edge of the sofa. My heart raced so fast I thought it would burst from my chest. I watched Violet's corkscrew hair stick straight out from her head, bouncing like golden springs. Rosalie Claire clutched my hand.

My stomach flopped and a flurry of candy and cards shot back down to the floor.

It was like a miracle. The plane was upright again.

And that's when things really took a turn for the worse. The cabin filled with the deafening wail of the engines, and the airplane shot upwards, high into the sky.

I could feel the taste of Froot Loops, sour milk, and puke creeping up my throat. *Please don't throw up, please don't throw up*, I chanted in my head. Mind over matter. Mind over matter. I shut my eyes and swallowed hard, forcing it all back down.

Rosalie Claire let go of my hand and unclipped her seatbelt. Inch-by-inch, she crawled to the bathroom door. She yanked hard on the handle but it wouldn't budge. Then she clung to it like a life raft as the plane rocketed upward.

I unbuckled my seatbelt.

"Son of a bee sting! What are you doing?" Violet hissed.

"Somebody's got to try and fix this thing!"

I clutched and crawled my way up toward Command Central. For every two feet of progress, I'd slip and slide back one. When I finally reached the controls, I hoisted myself up into Mike's pilot seat and clicked on the seatbelt. I grabbed the steering thingy. It was frozen into place.

On the instrument panel, strings of numbers flashed on and off faster than I could read. I touched the screen and the numbers reassembled into a series of letters, followed by a word that didn't surprise me one bit: *DANGER!*

With Mike locked in the bathroom, there was only one other person who could help.

"NOAH!" I screamed.

Noah must have already been on his way. An instant later he pulled himself into the co-pilot's seat and buckled up. His fingers frantically worked the controls. I'd never seen him look so fierce. His teeth clenched tight and his eyes bored down on the computer screen like a pair of gas-blue laser beams.

"Think, think, *think*." He sounded angry with himself for not figuring it out.

Higher and higher the plane rocketed into the stratosphere.

That's when I noticed something to the left of the screen.

"IS THAT A RESET BUTTON?" I shouted.

"TRY IT!" he yelled.

Would it turn off the plane and send us plummeting to the ground? Which fate would be worse? Shooting straight into outer space or crashing down to Earth?

I took my chances. With my pointer finger shaking, I reached over and hit the button. The computer shut off and flickered back to life. As the plane still shot upward, the following words appeared on the screen: *Steering yoke—deactivated. Elevator tail flaps down—locked. Bathroom door—locked.* Who in the world thought it was a good idea to design a plane with an automatically locking bathroom?!

Noah went to work. His fingers flew on the touch screen until the elevator tail flaps were up and the steering yoke was reactivated. The plane corrected its course and headed straight. Once again, the whining engines were whisper quiet.

That's when we heard the click of the bathroom door. Mike hurried out. His face was filled with relief and covered in sweat.

He took control of the plane, gently guiding it back down from the heavens. "I owe you kids. Guess the autopilot needs a tune-up."

Violet and Rosalie Claire rushed over and threw their arms around Noah and me in a giant group hug. Mike tried to join in.

"Please, just fly the plane," said Rosalie Claire. "There will be plenty of time for hugging later."

Mike gave a quick salute. "Roger that. And Noah? Madison? A million-and-one thanks."

"A million-and-one you're welcomes," I said as I felt my heartbeat returning to normal.

"Teamwork." Noah flashed a crooked grin.

It was just before noon when we touched down on a primitive grassy landing strip somewhere in the Brazilian jungle. I peered through the porthole window. As dangerous as the Amazon could be with its poisonous snakes and people-eating bugs, I decided this had to be a piece of cake compared to nearly flying straight into the sun.

Mike opened the hatch door and I was hit with the familiar jungle air. It was even thicker, hotter, and sweatier than Jacó. I was glad I'd remembered to pack bug spray.

"This is where you adventurers get off. Apologies for the technical glitches. Hugs?"

Everyone overlapped arms and pulled into a tight circle, touching head-to-head.

"Not that he'll believe me, but at least I'll have a great story to tell my little brother," Violet said as we collected our backpacks.

"See? There's a silver lining to everything!" Mike grinned.

"So, Mike?" Rosalie Claire asked. "Would you care to tell us what we're supposed to do now?"

"My pleasure. Walk upriver about three miles. You'll come to a lodge. Fabian is expecting you."

We scaled down the ladder. It felt good to be on solid ground.

"How will we get back to Jacó?" I asked. Not that I was hankering to hop on that flying deathtrap anytime soon.

"I have a feeling you won't be needing my services, Squirt. Catch you sometime in the future." With that, Mike yanked up the ladder and slammed the hatch door shut.

We watched the Astral plane cough and sputter as it flew up into the skies, back to heaven-knows-where.

Noah and I looked at each another and crossed our fingers.

"Here's hoping we're not stranded in the Amazon again," we said at exactly the same time.

CHAPTER TWELVE
Into the Amazon

We marched down to the water's edge and covered ourselves head to toe in bug repellant. I didn't want to be eaten by a bazillion insects, which can happen in the Amazon. Then we made our way single-file along the shore, beside the wide, lazy, caramel-colored river. As we headed east, we left our footprints in the spongy ground. A plastic bottle bobbed in the water. On its bleached-out label I could barely read the word *Stranded!* Obviously garbage left behind from the show.

"Noah, is this where we were last summer?"

"Sure looks like it," he said.

"I wish I'd been on that TV show with you guys." When Violet said it, I could tell she felt left out.

"You *think* you do, but you really don't," I told her.

"It was the weirdest thing I've ever done," Noah said. "I guess I can't complain since my dad and I won the million dollars, but some of those contestants were jerky."

"Well you two weren't. If I'd been on it, I would have given them a piece of my mind."

I had no doubt that's exactly what Violet would have done. She never had a problem telling people what she thought. Sometimes I wished I had guts to say what was on my mind the way Violet did, but I often worried I'd wind up hurting someone's feelings. Then I'd just clam up.

We'd been walking for over an hour when I heard a faint beep coming from my backpack.

"Hold up, guys!" I unzipped my pack and pulled out the GammaRay Particle Scanner. A cherry-red light flashed, matching the slow rhythm of the beeping sound. It meant that somewhere, not far from here, was the remote control for the MegaPix 6000! We all kept an eagle-eye lookout, although Noah said we couldn't be too close since the GPS wasn't beeping fast enough.

At last we spotted a sign on a wooden dock with letters made from glued-on twigs that said, "Tanini Lodge." As we stepped onto the rickety platform, four dolphins burst from the water in perfect half-moon arcs.

"Holy crab cakes! Those dolphins are *pink*!" Violet said.

Cotton candy pink, to be exact.

"They must be pink river dolphins. Their skin's so thin their blood shows through. Like they're constantly blushing." It was crazy how many cool facts Noah knew.

"I read somewhere the locals think they're magical," Rosalie Claire said.

I hoped that was true. We could use some magic right about now.

We followed Rosalie Claire up the narrow creaky wooden stairs to the lodge. Waiting at the top was a wiry Brazilian man with a hoop earring and a friendly smile.

"Good afternoon one and all! I am Fabian," he said in accented English. "I have been waiting for you! Follow me, please!"

Fabian led the way along a wooden catwalk past an open-air dining room, to a dozen huts built on platforms overlooking the river. He stopped at the last one on the end.

"Presenting your most excellent cabin!"

And it was. It looked like it could be a fairy's treehouse, hanging over the gurgling river. There were four canopied beds, one for each of us, and brightly painted wooden birds dangling from the thatched ceiling. Before he left, Fabian walked us out to the back deck where four hollowed-out pineapples were waiting, filled with cold fruit smoothies and jumbo straws. I took a long, slow sip. It was the most delicious thing I've tasted next to Rosalie Claire's blueberry pie.

It was then that I heard the muffled sound of the GPS in my backpack. I sucked down the rest of the smoothie lickety-split. The *beep-beep-beep* was a constant reminder that we needed to hurry and track down the remote before Florida got any sicker.

"Everybody ready?" I started for the door.

Violet slurped the last of her drink. "Bets on how long it'll take us to find it?"

"I vote for sometime before sunset," Noah said.

"From your mouth to God's ears," Rosalie Claire told him.

I pulled out the GPS and left my backpack on my bed. We let the beeps guide us deep into the jungle.

I'd forgotten how noisy the Amazon was. Howler monkeys bellowed. Frogs croaked. Mosquitoes buzzed in our ears. Birds screeched their warnings. As we trudged over twigs that snapped and crackled beneath our shoes, there was also an extra sound. The GammaRay Particle Scanner. As far as I could tell, it was beeping at exactly the same rate as it had when we'd arrived.

"Does anybody else think it's kind of creepy out here?" Violet slowed her pace, dropping behind Noah and me.

Wow. In my entire life, I've never seen Violet scared of anything.

"Don't worry. Usually the animals won't attack unless they're provoked." Noah's lips curled in a crooked smile.

"Gee, thanks," Violet said. "Then just make sure you don't let me step on any poisonous squirmy things."

We trudged through the Amazon, listening closely to the GPS and the jungle sounds, making our way over fallen logs and gnarled roots twisting above the ground.

It had been over an hour when Rosalie Claire stopped dead in her tracks.

"Listen!" she whispered.

We froze, struggling to figure out what we were supposed to hear. A vicious jaguar? A poison arrow frog? A deadly fer-de-lance?

"The GPS. Is it beeping faster?" she asked.

"Maybe," Violet said. "It's kind of hard to tell."

Violet was right. Were our ears playing tricks on us?

We kept walking. Noah and I were in the lead when a fluorescent green snake slithered past us through the decaying leaves. The next thing I heard was Violet's shriek, followed by Rosalie Claire's cry. Then BAM! I was knocked to the ground with a thud. Rosalie Claire had tumbled right on top of me.

Violet looked horrified. "Sorry, sorry, sorry! I was trying to get away from the snake."

"No worries. Let's blame it on the root I tripped on. Are you all right, Madison?" Rosalie Claire gave me her hand and helped me up.

"Yeah, I'm fine." I could feel a slightly scraped knee beneath my jeans. "What about you?"

"I think I heard something in my left ankle pop." Rosalie Claire sat back down and carefully worked off her boot and her sock. We watched her foot puff up like an inflatable pool toy. "Maybe I'll sit here a spell while you keep looking." She tried to move her ankle and winced in pain.

"No way," I told her. "We're taking you back to the lodge."

"Uh, Madison?" said Noah. "Where's the GPS?"

It was only then that I realized it wasn't in my hand. It must have flown from my grasp when I'd fallen.

Since Violet had been the one to knock down Rosalie Claire, she offered to stay with her while Noah and I hunted for the GPS.

We strained to hear the beeps, but the howler monkeys were riled up about something, so all we heard was their noisy squawking. Still, we searched every nook, cranny, bush, and tangled vine, trying hard to hear through the monkey racket.

At last I spotted the pulsing red light in a cluster of giant ferns. I crept closer. The sound was unmistakable. *Beep-beep. Beep-beep. Beep-beep.*

I dove in and grabbed the GPS. It definitely sounded faster! My heart pounded, keeping rhythm with the quickening beeps.

But finding the remote control would have to wait. The three of us helped Rosalie Claire hobble back through the jungle to the lodge. As the light faded, I kept wondering if the remote control had made its way out of the Amazon River. Where had it finally landed? It was all a big mystery. And it was one I planned to solve as soon as the sun came up the next morning.

CHAPTER THIRTEEN
Hot on the Trail

"I'm trusting you kids to stay safe," Rosalie Claire told us as I wrapped a towel packed with ice around her swollen ankle. Overnight her foot had turned plum purple.

"Promise," I said. "Are you *sure* you'll be OK?"

"I'll be fine. Fabian will take good care of me."

I hugged her goodbye and the three of us headed out to search for the missing remote. The sun was just rising, streaming fingers of light through skyscraper trees.

We charged down the wooden steps and rounded the corner of the lodge. The first thing we saw? A short man with hair the color of coal. He pulled a crate of vegetables from the back of a rusted white Jeep. What he wore made me stop dead in my tracks.

I nudged Noah and his eyes opened wide. "It looks like he's wearing the jacket Wolf Adams had on the first day of *Stranded in the Amazon*."

"Exactly," I said. "The one the monkey threw in the river with my remote control in the pocket." I'd recognize that jacket anywhere.

The vegetable man gave the box to the chef at the back door. Then he hopped into the driver's seat. The engine revved and mud splattered from the spinning tires.

"We gotta stop him!" Violet took off after the rattly Jeep. She was within spitting distance when it bounced away, down the mucky rutted road.

"Race you!" she yelled and broke into a sprint.

Noah and I ran after her. It wasn't long before the Jeep disappeared from sight. Breathing hard, we slowed down and followed the freshly laid tire marks in the mud. I watched Violet take in the dense forest thick with emerald green trees, skittering lizards, and chirruping birds. A huge smile spread across her face.

"Why was I such a boneheaded chicken yesterday? This place is *awesome*. Whoa! Check out the spider webs!" She scooted over to inspect an enormous cobweb on the spreading branches of a giant tree.

A big hairy spider was busy spinning an intricate pattern between leaves as big as hubcaps. Beads of dew clung to the silver threads and caught the light streaming down from the sun. The web looked as if it was studded with miniature pearls.

Then fast as anything, the light dimmed into semi-darkness, and the sky opened up with drenching rain. Enormous drops bounced off the ground like a bajillion SuperBalls. In five seconds flat, my t-shirt and jeans were soaked to my skin.

"Over here!" shouted Noah.

Violet and I sloshed through the mud to join him under nature's own umbrella—a canopy of giant palm fronds.

The rain stopped almost as fast as it had started, although at first it was hard to tell because of how much water still dripped from the trees. When it slowed, we scurried out from under our shelter.

The Jeep's tire tracks had washed away.

"This is a job for our handy-dandy GammaRay Particle Scanner." I pulled it from my backpack. It beeped, slow and steady.

We followed the makeshift road, cut between a forest of trees. The squishy mud turned our sneakers the color of hot cocoa. Just as the road stopped at a T, the beeps sped up. We had a decision to make.

I had a hunch which way we needed to turn. "Let's go right," I said. Violet had already turned left and was jogging at a steady pace. I called for her to stop so we could at least take a vote.

"Fifty-fifty chance it's this way, right?" Her voice was filled with the excitement of adventure.

But my gut told me we needed to go the opposite direction. I should have said something, although I didn't want to go against my best friend.

Noah shrugged and followed Violet. I gave in and brought up the rear.

The deeper we trudged down the path, the more I somehow knew we were heading the wrong way. It wasn't long before the GPS agreed with my intuition.

"The beeps are slowing down," I said.

"Positive?" asked Violet.

I held up the GPS as evidence.

"Madison's right. Let's head back." Noah turned around.

"Whatever. Can't win 'em all," she said and then clammed up. Violet never liked to be wrong.

We retraced our steps. Once we passed the T, the GPS beeped faster. We were definitely on the right track.

The beeping led us to a tiny village. A dozen wooden thatched-roof huts propped on stilts sat along a narrow river that branched off the Amazon.

Parked behind one of them was the rusty white Jeep.

The GPS went nuts. *Beep-beep-beep. Beep-beep-beep.* The remote control was so close I could practically feel it in my hands.

I knocked on the peeling whitewashed door of the hut closest to the parked Jeep.

No answer.

Because there weren't many houses in the village, I figured the vegetable man couldn't have gone far.

We made our way along the beach, past women sweeping the small covered porches of their homes, others tending vegetable gardens, and men patching boats along the shore.

We must have stuck out like three American sore thumbs. Whenever we passed someone, they'd first give us a curious look, then smile and say, *"Olá! Posso ajudá-lo?"*

I speak some Spanish but it sure didn't sound like Spanish to me.

"Brazilians speak Portuguese," Noah informed me.

At least some of it sounded *kind* of like Spanish. I was pretty sure they were saying hello and asking if we needed help. I just kept saying *olá* back and the three of us smiled and waved. If only I knew the Portuguese words for "vegetable man" and "safari jacket."

Just beyond the farthest hut beside the narrow river, we noticed a boy and a girl both about my age, hovering over a baby who wasn't more than a year old.

Beep-beep-beep-beep. Beep-beep-beep-beep.

"We're definitely getting warmer." Violet looked super excited and I was glad she was over her sulkiness.

My heart thumped faster with each beep of the GPS.

The two older kids glanced up, searching for the source of the sound.

"O que foi isso?" asked the boy, whose jet-black hair was choppy and short. He wore scruffy cut-offs and no shirt. A sleepy pet boa constrictor draped around his neck like a fat brown-speckled scarf.

He pointed to our beeping GPS and motioned for us to come closer.

Beep-beep-beep-beep-beep. Beep-beep-beep-beep-beep.

It *had* to be around here somewhere. I held up the beeping flashing gizmo so the snake boy could see it.

He stuck out one hand and pointed to his palm.

"Uh-oh. I think he wants us to give it to him." Violet looked worried, as if she thought the boy might steal it.

"I'm pretty sure he just wants to check it out," I said. "I think it'll be OK."

"Yeah, I have a feeling it'll be OK too," Noah said, which made me wonder if he had hunches just like me.

When I set the GPS down on the boy's outstretched palm, his eyes lit up. The girl, whose long licorice-black hair was as stick-straight as mine, wandered over to watch his finger trace over the red blinking light. He held the GPS against her ear and she winced from the stinging sound. That thing was seriously loud.

When the boy darted over to the baby and showed it to her, that's when I heard it.

Beep-beep-beep-beep-beep. Beep-beep-beep-beep-beep.

The baby's eyes grew wide with wonder and she giggled at the sight of the flashing light. She immediately dropped a plastic toy she'd been chewing on and snatched our GPS.

"Madison, look!" Noah pointed to the toy the baby had thrown on the ground.

It was the remote control for the MegaPix 6000!

CHAPTER FOURTEEN
Baby Troubles

Before I could grab the remote, the baby beat me to it. In one hand she clutched the GPS. In the other she held my remote control. It was a little scratched up, with tiny tooth marks indenting the hard plastic.

I crouched in the sand, eye-to-eye with the baby, and tapped the remote control. "This is mine. Sorry, you can't keep it." I shook my head, pointing first to me, and then to her. If she couldn't understand my words, then maybe she could figure out the universal signals for *mine* and *no way*.

I pointed to the beeping, blinking GPS in her other hand. "Yours," I said and smiled.

"Mmm-mm," she said, looking at one and then the other. I wondered if she was trying to figure out which one might be tastier.

"Pretty please?" I reached out my hand and tapped the remote again.

She said something in baby-speak and then dropped it in my palm. After that, she didn't pay an ounce of attention to me. She stared at the blinking red light and giggled. Then she popped one end of the GPS into her mouth like a lollipop.

The boy and the girl both smiled and seemed satisfied that the baby had something she wanted.

We waved goodbye to the trio and headed back the way we'd come.

"You're sure you want to let her keep that?" Violet asked.

"We're done with it. We got what we needed." I held up the remote for the MegaPix. Our round-trip ticket straight to the past.

The further away we got from the baby, the less the GPS would flash and beep. Soon it would fall silent. I wish there'd been a way to keep it working after we'd gone, but at least she had a brand new teething toy.

We hiked back toward Tanini Lodge. It must have been nearly noon. The sun was smack dab above the dense grove of towering trees.

"I'm starving," Noah said.

"Triple-starving," moaned Violet.

We'd left so early that we'd skipped breakfast. My stomach was grumbling too. I dug into my backpack and found three packets of Fruity Monkey Poop I'd stuffed in there before we'd left.

"Fruity Monkey Poop?" asked Noah. "What the heck?"

"Costa Rican delicacy," I said.

Violet grinned. "Sounds disgusting. I like it already."

Except it wasn't disgusting. It was gooey, sweet, and yummy.

Violet peered inside her packet. "Oh man! They're *gummies*!"

"You were hoping for the real thing?" I asked.

"Sure. I mean, how cool would it be to tell my brother that I ate genuine monkey poop?"

"There are tons of monkeys around here. If you really want some, I'm sure we could find you a nice fresh pile," I joked.

Violet screwed up her face. "Gross," she said and made a gagging sound. I guess she decided that the *idea* of eating real monkey poop was way more entertaining than eating it for real.

As we continued our trek, I noticed a cluster of bubblegum-pink flowering trees I hadn't seen before. "Hold on, guys. This place doesn't look familiar. Are we lost?"

"You might be right," Noah said. "We must have messed up. Let's turn around and go that way." He pointed back toward the village.

"Uh, hello? That's the wrong direction." Violet stared at Noah as if he were nuts.

"I know," he agreed. "But if we go back to the small river near the village and follow it, eventually it will lead us to the Amazon. Then we should be able to find the lodge. Or that's the theory anyway."

"You'd better be right. I'm not in favor of spending the night out here with poisonous snakes and piles of real monkey poop."

"If we're going to trust anyone in the great outdoors, it's Noah," I told Violet.

Noah grinned.

We followed him to the narrow river by the village and walked downstream along the shore for what seemed like forever.

"You guys *sure* this is right?" Violet asked.

I'd started wondering the same thing when we spotted the mouth of the river. It emptied right into the lazy wide Amazon.

We followed Noah along the river's edge, scrambling over vines and roots until, miracle of miracles, we caught sight of the Tanini Lodge.

"Brilliant! You did it!" I said, and the three of us high-fived.

"So you're a brain *and* a nature boy?" Violet looked impressed.

Noah's cheeks flushed red from the compliment. "My dad and I used to camp a lot."

Violet didn't know that before Noah and his dad won the million dollars on *Stranded in the Amazon*, they'd been dirt poor. To save money on rent, they'd camped every summer. It was bad news back then, although what Noah had learned during those summers was sure coming in handy now.

We raced back to the lodge to find Rosalie Claire up in our cabin, her swollen ankle packed in fresh ice that Fabian had brought. He'd also made her a pair of bamboo crutches.

"Any luck?" she asked.

I dug the remote from my backpack and held it up like a solid gold trophy.

"Well, well," Rosalie Claire said. "I'm not surprised. I had a feeling in my bones you'd find it."

Violet and Noah told her how I'd made a bargain with the baby. When they'd finished, I said it was time to go.

"Uh, any clue how we're getting back?" Violet asked.

I wasn't absolutely sure, but I had a pretty good idea. Or at least I hoped I did. "I think we're traveling by remote control."

OK, maybe I wasn't *a hundred percent* sure. I'd only zapped in and out of the MegaPix from a TV show, never from real life. I told my friends that we'd never know unless we tried.

CHAPTER FIFTEEN
Into the MegaPix

We pulled into a tight circle and held hands. Noah, Rosalie Claire on her crutches, Violet, and then me. With my free hand I positioned my thumb over the silver return button and the purple button.

"Hold on tight. Don't let go." I breathed deep and pushed.

Nothing happened.

"Uh, newsflash. We're still standing here," Violet said, pointing out the obvious.

Why wasn't it working? Suddenly, I got panicky. It had been *two days* since Dr. Morán had run those tests on Florida and I worried she was getting worse. The clock was ticking. How would we get home?

Then Noah asked the million-dollar question. He wondered if the MegaPix needed to be switched on before we could teleport back. I couldn't believe I hadn't thought of that myself.

"How in the world do we turn it on from here?" Violet asked. "Do you have a magic trick for that, Rosalie Claire?"

"Sorry, I don't, Violet. But I do have this." She pulled out her cell phone from her fanny pack and made a call. She asked Thomas to turn on the TV.

We held hands again. This time when I pressed the buttons I heard a familiar *ping*. My vision blurred, ice flowed through my veins, and lightning rocketed through my body. I held on extra tight to Violet and hoped everyone else was holding on tight, too.

The next thing I knew, we'd zapped back into the lobby of La

Posada Encantada. I heard the thumping of Leroy's tail. He leaped on me as if I'd been missing in action for weeks.

"Holy cow, that was insane!" Violet bounced from foot to foot.

"And *so* cool. It was like an ice storm and a wildfire in my body all at once." Noah patted his arms and legs, as if he was making sure his body had returned to normal.

When Thomas walked in wearing his food-splattered apron, his eyes twinkled at the sight of Rosalie Claire. "Thank the Lord you're back!" He hugged her tight and gave her a big kiss. "Holy mackerel, darlin'! What happened to your poor ankle?"

"It was just a silly accident. I'll be fine." She waved it away with the sweep of her hand.

"How's Florida?" I asked.

Thomas sighed. "Her fever spiked. One-hundred-and-four. I've been trying to keep it down with cold compresses and Tylenol."

Rosalie Claire took my hand and laced her fingers through mine. "The sooner you kids go see Grandma Daisy, the better."

"You're not coming?" I asked.

"With this poor ankle I'm afraid I'm out of commission. Besides, now I look twenty years older and if the folks I knew back then saw me, they might be terribly puzzled. And have no fear, my grandma will take excellent care of you."

Yes, maybe Grandma Daisy would take good care of us, but I knew we'd have to be extra careful to take good care of each other, too.

The three of us hurried to our hotel room to pack. It was hard to concentrate because I had only two things on my mind: meeting Grandma Daisy so she could fix the magic, and my mom. Would I see her in the past? I wanted that more than anything, so I triple-hoped I wouldn't be going back to a time when my grandmother had grounded her from going next door. According to my mom, that had happened *a lot.*

We gathered back in the lobby. Rosalie Claire unclipped her fanny pack and handed it to me. I slipped it into my backpack.

"Good luck, kids." Her brown sugar eyes sparkled. "You're going to do great."

"Thanks," I said, hoping she was right.

"Well? What are we waiting for?" Violet rubbed her hands together, excited enough to make sparks.

I was just as eager to go as Violet, but I told her there was one thing I needed to do first. I hurried to the yellow bungalow to see my grandmother.

She lay in the bed in my room. Her breathing was slow and raggedy. Her forehead was dotted with fever sweat, and she looked as if she was on death's doorstep.

"I'm going to get Rosalie Claire's fanny pack fixed so we can help you. Please hang on, Florida. Don't die on me like my mom, OK?" I whispered in her ear, even though she probably couldn't hear me. "Maybe things haven't been perfect between us, but I do love you. I really do." And then I kissed her goodbye.

Back in the lobby, Noah had already connected the video player to the MegaPix 6000.

When Violet slid Grandma Daisy's tape into the slot, I felt a swirling in my stomach. Even though Mike wasn't sure that we'd be able to travel into the past through the videotape, I crossed my fingers it would work the same way it did when I'd zapped into those TV shows. Besides, it *had* to work. How else could we save my grandmother?

"Rosalie Claire, what if we run into you in the past?" Noah wondered. "I've read a lot of sci-fi books and time travel can be tricky."

"You're right about that, Noah. Fortunately, I was off traveling the world in 1994. Besides, I have a funny feeling once you return to present time, the people you've run into in the past will forget they've met you. And kids? Be careful. The only person you should tell you're from the future is Grandma Daisy. She'll understand the magic. Anyone else might get awfully confused. And please, *please* don't do anything that will change the past. You don't want to risk impacting the future."

Noah nodded and pointed out something that sent shivers up my spine. "It's possible that if we change even one thing, you might never be born, Madison."

I gulped and promised we'd be super careful.

"And you'll make sure the MegaPix stays on and the video keeps running?" I asked Rosalie Claire.

"Honey, this TV will have a permanent babysitter until the three of you pop back out, safe and sound."

I know it sounds as if Rosalie Claire could be waiting in front of the TV for days and days, but it doesn't work like that. The tricky thing about TV teleporting is that when you zap into it, you're only gone for as long as the show is playing. If everything went as planned, we'd be away for no more than an hour since that's how long Grandma Daisy's tape took to play from beginning to end.

"Ready?" I asked my friends.

"Absolutely." Noah's eyes gleamed.

Violet pumped her fist in the air. "Let's do this thing!"

Noah hit PLAY on the VCR and the tape began to whirr.

I aimed the remote at the magic TV. Violet, Noah, and I held hands. Leroy whimpered, probably suspecting something was up.

When Grandma Daisy popped on the screen in her sunny yellow kitchen, my heart beat as fast as hummingbird wings.

I positioned my fingers over the enter button and the purple button, then pushed. *Ping!* Familiar words popped up on the screen.

*Are you **sure** you want to choose this channel? If "yes" push "enter" again.*

"Totally sure," I said.

"Here goes nothing," said Violet.

"Or here's goes *everything*, I hope," and crossed my fingers.

"Tell Grandma Daisy I love her and think about her every single day. And please, kids, hurry back."

"We will, Rosalie Claire," I promised.

Then I pushed enter again.

Ping!

The first thing I felt? My veins turning to ice. And the second thing? Leroy's front paws locking around my ankles.

We'd just turned the TV into a time machine and my dog was coming along for the ride.

CHAPTER SIXTEEN

Truth or Consequences, 1994

The next thing I knew, we were standing under the scorching sun next to my house in Truth or Consequences, New Mexico. Dusty gray rocks and clumps of dead brown grass dotted the bone-dry dirt in the yard. In front of us was Rosalie Claire's old sandy brown adobe house she'd inherited from Grandma Daisy. If things played out the way they were supposed to, Grandma Daisy was inside, recording her videotape.

Leroy let out a happy bark and sniffed every rock, snake hole, and scrubby weed in the yard. Then he wagged his tail. He was happy to be home.

"I think I figured it out!" Noah burst into a smile. "We must have passed through a wormhole in the space-time continuum!"

"Worms in space?" Violet looked as confused as I felt.

"No. Worm*holes*. Like an escape route in space from one time to another. The gamma rays in the remote and the TV caused our bodies to temporarily disintegrate. Then they turned us into a bunch of tiny molecules so we were small enough to travel through a wormhole to the past."

Wow, so *that's* how it worked? It would explain the feeling I had just before we popped into the yard. It was as if my body had splintered into a zillion little specks. Although I had to wonder . . . were we really in the past? So much looked the same. Rosalie Claire's backyard. The small adobe house. The clothesline strung between two metal poles.

Even the black rubber welcome mat at the back door. Was it possible that we were still in 2014?

"I need to check something out," I told my friends. I zipped the remote control into my backpack for safekeeping and headed next door to the red brick house. That's where my mom now lived, if we'd really traveled back in time. Was she at school? Or would she stare right at me if I peeked through the sliding glass door? Then what would I do? Was I even ready for that? Or what if we weren't in the past after all? Would I see my present-day Grandpa Jack, scratching his head, wondering where Florida had gone?

I came down with an instant case of the jitters. My heart jackhammered harder and harder the closer I got to the house.

"Wait, this is where you live?" asked Violet, who had never visited me in Truth or Consequences.

"Yep," I said.

Leroy padded behind us, still sniffing, his nose twitching fast as a rabbit's. He trotted to the door and scratched. Under no circumstances would I be letting him in.

"Maybe you guys should look first," I whispered.

"What'll we do if your mom's in there?" Noah asked, and I wondered if he'd read my mind.

"I don't know." My voice was hoarse and my head felt full of cotton.

Violet volunteered and scooted to the sliding door. She pressed her face against the glass. "Coast is clear. No one's home. I bet she's at school." She sounded disappointed, although I wasn't. Even though I'd been wishing to see my mom one more time, all of a sudden I didn't have a clue what I'd say to her if we actually came face-to-face. I worried I'd blurt out the truth, which could change everything. Like the fact that I was born.

I peeked into the living room and couldn't believe my eyes. Everything was different. In place of Florida's red velvet sofa was one with giant orange flowers. Gold-framed mirrors hung everywhere, and the shelves that would someday be filled with her shopping show knick-knacks were nowhere to be seen.

Crash! Clang! BOOM! We jumped at the sharp sound of clattering metal.

Leroy cowered behind my legs.

It was our neighbor Manny. He was in his backyard, right behind Florida's house, tossing a truck bumper onto a junk heap. Now *there* was a difference. In the future, Manny would have cast-off computers in piles everywhere, but now his yard was littered with car parts. And there was no doubt about it: Manny definitely looked a whole lot younger. Even though he was still skinny as a plank and wore his dark hair slicked back smooth, he didn't have a single wrinkle crisscrossing his face. Now I was absolutely sure we'd really gone back to the past.

Manny kicked a metal drum with his boot and shouted a nasty word. OK, that part about the guy was exactly the same.

Leroy whimpered and shook with fear.

"Don't worry, boy. No one's going to make you live with mean old Manny again." I stroked Leroy's head.

My dog had once belonged to Manny who was the Worst Pet Owner in Recorded History. Last summer, when my Grandpa Jack bought Leroy from him for a hundred dollars, it was the happiest day of my life. And Leroy's, too.

Manny's back screen door slammed shut and everything turned quiet again. The enormity of our situation sent a flurry of questions rocketing around my brain.

Was Grandma Daisy really and truly inside Rosalie Claire's old house? If she was, would she be able to fix the fanny pack? Then if she did fix it, would the magic be strong enough to save my grandmother?

And what if I bumped into my mom while I was in the past? Should I try to stay away from her so I wouldn't run the risk of changing the future?

CHAPTER SEVENTEEN
Grandma Daisy

I inhaled some courage, mounted the steps to the back porch, and knocked three times on the door.

No answer.

"Maybe she's out," Violet said.

"But we traveled through the MegaPix. She was on the videotape when we zapped in. She should be here. At least that's how it worked with the TV shows."

"Try it again," Noah said.

I knocked once more. Leroy got bored and waddled to his favorite spot in the shade of the lone cottonwood tree, which I suddenly realized was much smaller than it would be when I moved here nearly twenty years in the future.

The door sprung open and Grandma Daisy stood on the other side, all chocolate skin, smile wrinkles, and twinkly brown eyes. And she was short. Almost exactly my height and I wasn't nearly done growing.

"Well, look who's here." She was just as sparkly as she'd been in the video.

Had she been expecting us?

My friends and I exchanged looks of complete confusion.

"I'm Madison," I gulped. "These are my friends, Violet and Noah. And my dog, Leroy."

"It looks like Leroy has made himself at home."

Leroy was busy digging for bones that he probably remembered burying under the tree, years in the future.

"Of course, I didn't know what your names would be, but last night I had a dream that Rosalie Claire was sending three visitors my way. And a cat. Of course, I don't always get everything right in my dreams." Her eyes crinkled into a smile.

Holy cow! Rosalie Claire always said her Grandma Daisy was magic. Could she dream the future too?

"We need to talk. It's important," I said.

"Of course, dear. That was also part of the dream."

"OK, you might think this is super weird. I hardly believe it myself," I began.

"Tell me. So little surprises me anymore."

"We're from the future. From 2014." I felt as if I'd just stepped into a corny science fiction movie as I told her all about the MegaPix 6000 and how the remote control zapped us here through the wormholes.

"Oh my. I've always had visions about traveling to the future." Her eyes twinkled at the thought.

"Rosalie Claire wanted me to make sure to tell you that she sends her love and thinks about you every day. We've been visiting her and her husband Thomas in Costa Rica where they live," I said.

"My granddaughter is married? How wonderful! Why that news alone makes your visit extra-special! Is her Thomas a kind and loving man?"

I nodded. Then without warning, my eyes welled up with tears.

"Oh dear. Here I am prattling on about my granddaughter and I can see you haven't come on a simple visit. What's wrong, child?"

I stared at the dirt. My words stuck in my throat.

Violet came to my rescue and draped her arm over my shoulder. "Madison's grandma is real sick and Rosalie Claire's fanny pack stopped working. She said you'd know how to recharge it."

"Oh dear. What's wrong with your grandmother?"

I wiped my eyes. "It's a strange jungle disease the doctors haven't figured out. I'm worried Florida could die."

"My goodness!" Grandma Daisy's hand flew to her mouth. "Wait a minute. Are you saying that Florida is your *grandmother*? Florida Brown?"

I nodded.

"My stars, then you must be Angela's daughter. I did not get that right in my dream at all and it's the most important part. Now I know why you look so familiar. I'd know that silky brown hair and your beautiful smile anywhere."

It's true. Parts of me looked exactly like my mom.

"I brought the fanny pack. Can you recharge it?" I asked.

"Oh my, I do hope so." Then it was Grandma Daisy's turn to stare down at the dirt, as if she was trying to puzzle something out. "You know, maybe we should all go inside for a nice cold drink. There's someone inside I'd like you to meet."

Who would it be? My throat turned dry and I swallowed hard.

"And it looks as if your dog could use something tastier than a mouthful of dusty stones."

I turned back to the cottonwood tree and saw Leroy gnawing on rocks, probably wondering why they didn't crunch like buried bones.

When I called for him, he scampered up the steps behind us and we all went into the house.

The first thing I noticed in Grandma Daisy's kitchen was the calendar we'd seen in the video. And the second thing? A tripod stood on the pine floor with no video camera attached to it.

"This way," said Grandma Daisy.

We followed her into the living room. A girl sat on the sofa, ejecting a videotape cassette from a camera. Her straight brown hair grazed her shoulders, just like mine. She wore a Bart Simpson t-shirt and cut-off jean shorts.

Grandma Daisy cleared her throat. "I'd like you kids to meet my good friend and cameraperson extraordinaire, Angela Brown."

I nearly fainted. It was my mother. And she wasn't much older than me.

CHAPTER EIGHTEEN
My Kid-Mom

"Hey!" my mom said. "What's your name?"

She was talking to me. My mouth felt like it was stuffed with balled-up socks. I couldn't say a word and I couldn't stop staring. Shouldn't she know me? OK, so maybe I hadn't *technically* been born yet, but she was still my *mom*.

Even though she couldn't have been more than fourteen, I would have recognized her anywhere. She had the same light-brown gold-flecked eyes, and the same wide smile as her grown-up self. My kid-mom even had the sea of freckles covering her arms where she used to let me use colorful washable markers to play connect-the-dots. There was something so familiar about her. A spark and a spirit that could only belong to my mother.

I did everything in my power to fight back an avalanche of tears and stop myself from rushing into her arms. How weird would that be? When I'd first double-wished that I could see her one more time, I hadn't imagined she'd be a kid just like me.

Grandma Daisy slipped her arm around my waist. "Angela, this is Madison. And these are her friends, Violet and Noah."

Leroy trotted over to my mother and sniffed every inch of her like he'd just found a treasure chest filled with beef bones. He nuzzled his head in her lap.

"Cool dog. What's your name, boy?"

"Leroy," I said. My voice sounded like a squeaky toy.

"I wish I could have a dog. One of the many things on my mother's *Not in This Lifetime* list." She snapped the VHS tape into the plastic container and wrote the words "Daisy's Special Remedies" on the label with a black Sharpie.

Noah nudged me to make sure I'd noticed.

"Did you guys just move into the neighborhood?" she asked.

How could I possibly tell my mom where I lived? Next door, in her house, twenty years in the future?

"Noah lives in Denver. Madison and I are from Bainbridge Island, near Seattle," Violet said, covering for me.

"An island? That's totally awesome! Why would you come to T or C?" She said it as if Truth or Consequences was the worst place on Earth.

Don't tell her the truth, or you could mess up everything, I reminded myself. But what *should* I say? Before I could think something up, Grandma Daisy jumped in.

"Rosalie Claire met them on her travels. She thought they'd enjoy a visit during their school vacation."

As much as I *hate* lying, in this case it was definitely better than telling her that in the future she was going to be my mom.

"Nice! You must have a late spring break. Are you guys staying here with Daisy?"

Were we? I had no idea.

"Of course they are. I was thinking they might like to go to Fiesta this weekend."

Fiesta was a celebration that happened every year at the beginning of May. The town would fill up with tourists, food booths, and carnival games. It all kicked off with practically half the people who lived here marching down Main Street in a big parade.

"Sweet! We'll be neighbors, at least for a little while. Hey, I'm going to videotape the parade. You should come with me. Fiesta's the bomb." My mom popped the plastic cap onto the camera lens.

Sweet? The bomb? Wow, she sure had the teenage language thing down back when she was a kid.

We were interrupted by a familiar scream coming from next door. "Angela Brown, get your scrawny butt home this instant!"

I shook my head. "Florida," I said before I could catch myself.

"You know my mother?" My kid-mom looked completely confused. I felt my face blushing red.

This time it was Noah who came to my rescue. "No, Rosalie Claire told us all about her. Isn't that right, Madison?"

I nodded and felt like kicking myself. I'm a terrible liar. This time-travel cover-up business was going to test my soul.

"Gotcha. Well, sounds like my mother just got back from her Red Hot Mamas Club meeting, so I gotta go. I get to find out what she and her stupid friends are wearing for this year's parade. Whatever it is, I'm sure it will be totally embarrassing."

"Good luck," I said.

"Let's hang out sometime, except not when my mother's around. She can be a total pain in the you-know-what."

Florida yelled for her again. My mom smirked, then dragged her feet out the back door and down the steps.

"That was your *mother*?" Violet said the second she was gone. "How *Freaky Friday* is that?"

I was in shock. I collapsed onto the sofa right on the spot where my mom had been sitting. It was still warm.

"All things considered, you did well," Grandma Daisy said. "Know what I think? I think we all need some lemon balm lavender iced tea to calm our jangly nerves." She went off to the kitchen.

"I guess she looks *sort* of the same. And kind of like you," Violet said. "Holy Toledo, it's so *weird*."

Weird was an understatement. The whole experience made my head hurt and my heart ache.

"Tea's ready!"

Grandma Daisy set four tall glasses of ice-cold tea on the kitchen table. It was sweetened with what she said was a special calming honey made with chamomile flowers. On the floor was a bowl of ice water for Leroy.

I pulled the fanny pack from my backpack and set it on the table in front of Grandma Daisy. "Rosalie Claire said you have a piece of amber with a frog in it that will recharge the magic."

She sipped her tea through a straw and was quiet for just a little too long. "I used to have that piece of amber," she finally said.

"Used to?" asked Noah.

"Until it went missing."

"*Missing?*" Noah, Violet, and I said it at the same time.

"For years I kept it tucked away at the Wildflower and used it to strengthen magic that had grown weak. One day it up and disappeared. I've always had a nagging feeling that a man named Walter Brinker stole it. It happened not long after I sold him his own fanny pack. Black leather, if I recall."

"Do *you* have a fanny pack, Grandma Daisy?" I asked.

"Oh my, yes. The poor little thing grew so threadbare I sent it off for patching and re-stitching. The fellow's had it for nearly three weeks. Otherwise I could have used your remote thingamabob to go into the future and fix Florida myself." Grandma Daisy sighed. "If my hunch is right and Walter has the amber, he holds the only cure I know for Rosalie Claire's pouch."

And the only salvation for Florida.

"Well then, we're just going to have to find Walter Brinker and ask him." Violet finished her last drop of tea with a noisy slurp.

"Where does he live?" Noah asked.

"On the edge of town behind the Shell station. Although I don't know how I feel about sending you three there."

"Why?" I asked.

Grandma Daisy sighed. "Walter Brinker is a grumpy recluse. I'm not sure you should be poking around his life."

"But we're the Mighty Trio." Violet lifted both fists in the air like a winning prizefighter. "Three against one. And four against one if you come with us."

Grandma Daisy shook her head. "I'm afraid I'd do you more harm than good. I've tried talking with him. The man won't give me the time of day."

On the other hand, that didn't mean Walter Brinker wouldn't talk to *us*.

I made a vow right then and there that until I tracked down that amber and recharged Rosalie Claire's fanny pack, I wasn't leaving 1994.

CHAPTER NINETEEN
Mom's Florida Problems

That night we helped Grandma Daisy pull a pile of fluffy blankets and soft feather pillows from her leather trunk.

"Sweet Mother Pickles, that's the same trunk Rosalie Claire has at La Posada Encantada."

"Perhaps it is, Violet. Maybe I give it to her in the future." Grandma Daisy spread three futons on the living room floor.

After a canopy of stars appeared like diamonds in the night sky, we settled into our makeshift beds. When I slept, I dreamed my mom was back to her grown-up self. We were in our old house on Bainbridge Island and she held a glowing amber orb as big as a soccer ball. I pressed my palms against it and together we zapped to the beach in Costa Rica. She sat cross-legged on the sand and watched me surf while I waited for the perfect wave. I wanted to show her how much I'd learned that summer. A championship swell rose up and I rode it to shore, my surfboard flying three feet above the water. When I looked to see if she was watching, my mom smiled at me and grew thin as fog. Then she rose up to join the clouds drifting above the sea.

I awoke to the sound of a heavy pan banging on the stove.

"I totally *hate* her." My kid-mom sounded as if she was trying not to cry.

"Hate is a bitter word," Grandma Daisy said. "It's poison for your heart."

"I know, I know," is what I think my mom replied, except her voice was almost too whispery to hear.

But the amazing thing? What Grandma Daisy had said to my mom about hate being poison is *exactly* what my mom used to say to me.

My friends were still sleeping, so I tiptoed into the kitchen. Grandma Daisy and my mom were making pancakes. Leroy sat at attention by the stove, his stumpy tail ticking side to side as he waited hopefully for a stray morsel to fall at his feet.

"Oopsie!" Grandma Daisy accidentally-on-purpose lobbed a pancake over her shoulder.

Leroy's tail wagged double time and he inhaled it before it even hit the floor.

"Good morning," I yawned.

"Hey, we're making banana-blueberry pancakes before school." My mom poured small circles of batter into the big cast iron skillet. "Hope your night was better than mine."

"Why? What happened?"

"You know the parade I promised I'd take you guys to? The one I was going to videotape? Now I can't. My Mother the Witch is making me ride with her little group of Red Hot Mamas and their daughters on their dumb float."

"We could come watch you," I said.

"No way. You'd laugh if you saw me. Fiesta is a circus theme this year and so what does my mother buy for me to wear? A totally butt-ugly baby pink tightrope walker costume. It looks like somebody barfed all over it with a mouthful of glitter."

"Ouch. Sounds gross."

"I know, right? What mother makes their kid do stuff like that? I bet yours doesn't."

My eyes flicked over to Grandma Daisy who hesitated before slipping the browned pancakes onto a plate in the warm oven.

"She'd never do anything like that. My mom was the coolest mom on the planet," I said.

"*Was?* Did something happen to her?"

The oven door banged and I jumped. I swear the *thump-thump* of my heart sounded louder than the *tick-tock* of the kitchen clock.

"I, uh, mean she *is* the coolest mom on the planet." Because there was no denying that my mother was standing right there in front of me. And she did seem pretty darn cool.

"You know what? I'm not going on that stupid float. Period. She can't make me."

With Florida, I knew it was usually her way or the highway. If my mom refused, my grandmother would probably ground her. If that happened, I might never get to see her again.

"You still have a few days before the parade," I said hopefully. "Maybe she'll change her mind." In my year-and-a-half of living with Florida I knew that if I waited her out, every once in a while she'd come around to seeing things my way.

"Yeah, that's not going to happen. My mother's brain is made of cement. She changes her clothes three times a day, but she never changes her mind."

It sounded as if Florida had been even more of a pain when my mom was growing up.

Violet and Noah wandered in and we all ate breakfast, then the three of us changed out of our PJs.

Grandma Daisy found a rope that we used as a leash for Leroy and the five of us plus my dog headed into town. The whole time my mom stayed right by my side.

"Hey, I like your red bird necklace."

"Thanks. It's a firebird." I held the charm between my thumb and my finger and flew it back and forth on the chain. I wasn't sure if I should tell her that it was a gift from Rosalie Claire, so I decided it would be best to keep the information to myself.

"Maybe you could get one someday," is what I did say, since I knew for a fact that it wouldn't be long before Rosalie Claire would give my mom one of her own.

"That would be the bomb. I totally love it."

We turned onto Broadway. The town of Truth or Consequences was almost frozen in time. Not much looked different twenty years ago except that the cars were older. And a guy wearing a backwards baseball cap walked down the street yelling into a cell phone that was big enough to be one of those landline telephones some people have in their houses. Just as it would be in the future, the sleepy street was filled with dusty stores selling second-hand cast-offs.

My mom stopped and said goodbye. "Wish I could play hooky from school today. Catch you guys later." I watched her disappear around the corner, her navy blue backpack sagging with books.

We followed Grandma Daisy to the Wildflower Mercantile, the shop she owned on Main Street. She pushed open the door and we followed her inside. I held my breath. Whenever I'd go into the store in the future, it always stunk of incense, dust, and dead mice. Although the second I stepped inside, I realized that now the scents were heavenly. Lavender, sage, nutmeg, and honeysuckle filled my nostrils. One wall was lined with jars packed with mysterious herbs like fawn's breath, fireweed, and feverfew. The whole place glistened with sparkly crystals, gold metal amulets, ancient arrowheads, crystal balls, and small green antique scarabs that looked like beetles turned to stone. Every square inch was chock-full of magical treasures.

"Madison, Violet, Noah? I'd like you to meet my friend Mike." Grandma Daisy gestured toward a young redheaded guy working behind the counter.

It was Mike. Magic TV Mike. *My Mike.*

CHAPTER TWENTY
Mike

"Mike's my main man around here. And a lifesaver since I've cut back on my working hours," Grandma Daisy told us.

"Nice to meet you," I said and we each shook his hand.

Mike didn't seem to know me. Which made sense since this was ages before the delivery of the MegaPix 6000. In his mind, today was the first time we'd ever met.

But the most bizarre thing? He appeared to be almost the same age he was the day he first delivered the magic TV. How was that even possible?

The second he went off to help a customer and was out of earshot, Violet bet me that this Mike wasn't our Mike at all. She thought it was more likely that it was his father.

"Except didn't Rosalie Claire say she knew our Mike back when Grandma Daisy ran this place?" I whispered back.

"If you do the math, then MegaPix Mike hasn't been born yet," Noah said. "I think Violet is right. This guy probably is his dad. Rosalie Claire could have easily met your Mike back when he was a little kid, right?"

He had a good point. So that would make MegaPix Mike, Mike *junior*. And even though it made perfect sense, they looked almost like twins to me, minus the scruffy beard.

Leroy, who'd been busy biting his butt, finally noticed Mike. My dog trotted over and nudged his blue jeans until he earned himself a scratch on the head. I wondered if Leroy thought he looked just like our Mike too.

After he finished up with his customer, Grandma Daisy explained that we were looking for the missing frog amber and how we wanted to pay a visit to Walter Brinker. Thankfully, she didn't mention we'd come from the future.

"So, Mike," Grandma Daisy asked, "a penny for your thoughts?"

"I make it a point never to trust a guy who's only fifty percent honest," he said.

Grandma Daisy let out a big sigh. "That was my worry too. That's why I wanted your opinion."

"You know what?" Noah said. "Dealing with Walter Brinker couldn't be any scarier than shooting down an out-of-control river in a flashflood, or being attacked by bugs the size of baseballs, which is what Madison and I did last summer."

"Oh my!" Grandma Daisy's eyebrows arched in surprise, wrinkling up her forehead.

"Impressive." Mike let out a long low whistle.

"And we lived to tell the tale. We really need to do this," I said.

Grandma Daisy drummed her fingers on the glass countertop. She looked at us one by one, her eyes narrowed in thought.

"Yes, I know that," she said. "Which is why you should go see him. I have a feeling in my bones that you kids can handle this. Unfortunately, I don't drive any more. I wrecked one too many cars when my mind wandered off the road and onto other things."

"I can give them a lift," Mike offered. "Although they might be wasting their time."

He disappeared into the storeroom to get his keys. It gave me time to ask Grandma Daisy the question that nagged me the second we'd walked through the door.

"Does Mike have a son?"

"Oh, heavens to Betsy, no."

"What is he, like twenty or something?" Violet asked.

"He certainly looks that young to me," said Grandma Daisy. "Although I'm never very good with telling folks' ages."

If Mike was twenty, that would make him about the same age as MegaPix Mike. Maybe Violet and Noah were right. This Mike could become the dad to the man who winks at me and calls me Squirt.

We hopped into Mike's old sky-blue Toyota. As it sputtered down the street I'm sure the sound of my heartbeat drowned out the *clunk-clunk-clunk* of the engine. Would Walter Brinker be as creepy as I thought?

"When we get the amber, then do we just go home?" asked Violet. "Because I think we should at least hang out for Fiesta. It sounds like a blast."

"We might have to leave before that, Violet." I shot her a look, hoping she could read my mind. After all, we were here to find a cure for Florida, not to wait around just so we could eat junk food and play carnival games. Although one thing I knew for sure? I wouldn't leave the past before seeing my mom again.

"Where is home, anyway?" asked Mike.

"Bainbridge Island, near Seattle," said Violet.

"Denver," said Noah.

"Home is where the heart is." I tried to make it sound like a joke because no way could I tell him the real story.

"Now isn't that the honest truth?" Mike winked at me in the rearview mirror.

OK, that was definitely Mike's wink. How weird was it that my Mike and his dad winked in the exact same way? But there were things about Rosalie Claire and Grandma Daisy that were the same too. Like the fact that they both said they felt things "in their bones."

On the edge of town, we passed two men in shorts and tank tops smacking hammers on what looked like a parade float. It was a small version of a circus big top on the back of a flatbed trailer. An almost life-sized papier-mâché elephant stood on the sidewalk, its trunk lifted in a soundless trumpet. Leroy took one look at the fake elephant and went nuts, barking his head off. He squished his wet nose against the window, trying to smell the elephant through the glass.

"Looks like somebody else is interested in checking out the Fiesta parade on Saturday," Mike joked.

We drove two miles out of Truth or Consequences to an old Shell gas station I knew wouldn't be there in the future. Mike kept his motor running. Before I'd moved here, the place must have been knocked down, which probably could have been done with a swift kick. The adobe walls were crumbling and the plate glass window was cracked. It's amazing the building could stand at all.

"You want to come with us?" Noah asked Mike.

"No thanks. Walter's not exactly the president of my fan club. He wouldn't talk to Daisy or me if we paid him."

"Fingers crossed he talks to us," I said.

"Miracles can always happen. Call me from the pay phone when you're ready to be picked up." Mike wrote his number on a paper scrap and handed it to me.

"Thanks." I stuffed it in my pocket and we piled out of the car. I tied the rope to Leroy's collar.

"By the way, if the old codger has the amber, he has to give it up willingly or the magic won't work. Even magic has its rules." Mike saluted and we watched his car putter back down the highway.

We crossed the road to the gas station. It looked deserted. No cars were filling up with gas and nobody was working out front. We peered through the broken window into a small dingy office. A greasy jacket hung on a metal folding chair and Styrofoam cups were strewn around the desk.

"Hello! Anybody here?" I called.

"Hey, check it out. The coffee's still hot." Noah pointed to the cup by the phone. Curls of steam rose in the air.

Kabang! Kabang! Kabang!

"What the heck?" The sound was so loud it made my ears ring.

"It's coming from out back," Violet said.

We followed her behind the gas station. Next to a rusty doublewide trailer propped up on bricks stood a man in overalls.

I took one look at him and froze. "Guys, he has a gun!"

CHAPTER TWENTY-ONE
Outfoxing Walter Brinker

Rapid fire, the man shot his BB gun at a line-up of tin cans.

Kabang! Kabang! Kabang!

"Bet that's him. Come on." Violet started in his direction.

I grabbed her arm. "No way! Do you want to get shot?"

There's not a lot I'm scared of, although if I were making a list, guns would be at the very top.

Kabang! Kabang! Kabang!

Leroy growled and pulled so hard on his rope leash that it yanked from my hand. He hightailed back toward the gas station.

"Leroy, sit!" I commanded.

He dropped his butt on the dirt, missing a spiky cactus by an inch.

At the sound of my voice, the man whirled around. Even though he was round as a dumpling, his oily overalls were two sizes too big. His dirty brown hair was slicked to the side by its own grease. Cinched around his waist was a black fanny pack.

"You got no business bein' here if you're not buyin' gas." He aimed his BB gun at our feet and spat on the dirt.

Leroy slinked to my side and I grabbed his collar. He let out a snarl and the man turned his gun on him.

I took a deep breath. "Please sir, don't shoot my dog. He's nervous around loud noises."

"It's only a dang BB gun. Now git that dog to clap his trap."

I shushed Leroy and he cowered between my legs.

"What do you little varmint stains want?" His voice sounded even growlier than Leroy's.

"Um, are you Walter Brinker?" I had to force my voice above a whisper.

"That's me. Who's askin'?"

"I'm Madison McGee. These are my friends, Violet and Noah."

Walter stared at us and said nothing.

"Uh, I wanted to tell you that's a really cool fanny pack you're wearing. I bet you find a lot of great stuff in there." I was hoping I could butter him up.

Walter snorted. "Yeah right. I wish." Which made me wonder if something might be wrong with his pack. "Who sent you here anyway?" His beady eyes squinted into slits.

"Nobody. We're here because we need your help."

"What kinda help? You're too young to drive so you can't be lookin' to fix a flat tire."

"We're trying to find a piece of ancient amber," Noah told him.

"One with a dead frog in it," Violet added.

"Then you're sniffin' in the wrong hole. Now why don't all of you git before my trigger finger gets itchy?"

The three of us backed off fast, but Leroy had something else in mind. He spotted a jackrabbit and pulled from my grasp. With a yelp, he streaked straight past the house and across the desert in hot pursuit.

"That mutt of yours is so dumb he couldn't teach a hen to cluck. Go git him and then git home."

Walter stomped over to a copper-colored van parked beside his doublewide. He reached through the window and pulled out a rifle. A real gun. With real bullets. Like the kind that can kill you in a single shot. He slammed the gun's butt hard on the dirt and fired us another death stare.

"Sorry, please don't shoot," I cried before racing around to the back of the trailer. I charged deep into the desert, calling for Leroy.

When Leroy finally lost sight of the rabbit and gave up the chase, he trotted back to me. I grabbed his rope leash, tied a strong loop, and slipped it over my wrist. Together we hurried toward Walter's trailer. A glint in the window caught my eye.

"Come on, boy," I whispered.

We crept closer. That's when I heard the front door slam. Walter was inside.

My knees shook as I crouched below the window. What I saw made me gasp. A smooth nugget of golden amber on the sill shimmered in the sunlight. Trapped inside was a tiny dead frog.

Pulling Leroy on the rope, I raced to the front of the trailer, straight to Violet and Noah.

"I found it! The amber's inside his house!"

Next thing I knew, Violet was pounding on the front door.

"What are you doing?" I hissed.

"Getting it back."

"Are you sure that's a good idea?" asked Noah.

Violet knocked until her knuckles turned red. I crossed my fingers that all that knocking wouldn't bug Walter so much that he'd yell at us, or worse. In the end, he refused to answer the door.

We headed back to the front of the gas station to hatch a plan.

Noah noticed the long rubber hose stretched on the asphalt in front of the gas tanks. "Wow. You don't see those old things every day. You know what? If a car drives over that hose it'll ding. Then Walter will *have* to come out."

"Boy genius at work," said Violet.

We leaned against the gas pumps and waited almost an hour for someone to pull into the station. We counted eighty-eight cars and every single one of them zipped on by.

"This is getting boring," Violet complained.

"Super boring," I agreed. It was time to take matters into my own hands. Or, make that my own *feet*. I got up and jumped on the rubber hose, trying to coax out a ding.

No luck.

"You don't weigh enough," Noah pointed out.

So the three of us positioned our feet on the hose.

"One. Two. Three. Jump!" Violet chanted.

We jumped.

Nothing.

We tried again.

Zero, zippo, zilch.

"We could hold something heavy," Noah suggested.

We scanned the area around the gas station. The weight of the empty cans and bottles littering the ground wouldn't have added up to a bag of beans.

"How about Leroy?" I asked. My dog wasn't gigantic, but he was brick solid.

"Great idea," Violet agreed. The two of us hoisted him up, his round belly straddling our arms. "He's *heavy*," she grunted. "Let's do this quick."

Noah counted to three and we all jumped.

DING!

After a few minutes Walter swaggered up, expecting a customer. The second he spotted us I could hear him grumble.

It wasn't the pleading looks on our faces or even Leroy's smile that flipped Walter's switch. It was Noah. "Mr. Brinker, how's that fanny pack working for you? Giving you everything you need?"

"What do you know about it, boy?" Walter sneered and narrowed his eyes.

"Not much. But Madison does. Give us ten minutes of your time.

You never know. You might learn as much from us as we do from you. Ten minutes. That's all we're asking."

Walter peered at us, one by one. "OK, crumb-crunchers. You can come in. But don't be expectin' no miracles."

CHAPTER TWENTY-TWO
Let's Make a Deal

Deer heads and old guns decorated the walls of Walter's wood-paneled living room. They gave me the creeps. Over a potbelly woodstove hung a framed saying stitched in needlepoint: *Even a blind squirrel finds an acorn now and then.* On a bookshelf stood a silver-framed photograph of a teenaged couple dressed for the prom. Next to it was a neat stack of books by Louis L'Amour. By the looks of them, they were all stories about cowboys. Even though the room was crammed with stuff, everything had its place.

We stood awkwardly in the doorway, unsure of what to do.

"Go on. Sit your butts down," Walter said, and chose an overstuffed chair for himself.

I went straight for the wooden stool under the window where I'd spotted the amber.

It was gone. The only thing left was a ring of dust.

"Mighty interested in that window ledge, are ya?"

"Uh, I just thought I'd check on Leroy."

Before he'd let us in the house, Walter had made us tie Leroy up outside.

"Your mutt's in front, not out back. And I know what you're after, so don't try pullin' the wool over my eyes."

Busted. My stomach tied up in a hard knot. My eyes flicked around like one of those cat clocks with a wagging tail. It's what always happens when I lie, which is hardly ever. I'd thought maybe this situation had qualified as a special circumstance, when being dishonest would be OK, but I was wrong.

So, as usual, the truth was best. I moved the stool next to Violet and Noah, and sat in front of Walter Brinker, face-to-face. "Mr. Brinker, I know you have the piece of amber with the frog in it. I need it. It's a matter of life or death."

Walter squinted at me, cold and hard.

"Are you sure that lil' old hippie lady from the Wildflower didn't send you to sniff me out?" Walter tapped one of his wrinkled leather cowboy boots on the brown-speckled linoleum floor.

"She didn't send us *exactly*," I said. "She told us it was *possible* you had the frog amber and we asked her where you lived."

"We insisted," said Noah.

"Begged, actually," added Violet.

"Well, sorry to stomp on your campfire, Missy, but that little piece of rock ain't what it's cracked up to be."

"Great!" Violet said. "I guess that means you don't really need it."

"I didn't say that, now did I?" Walter growled. "It's the only thing that makes my pouch here worth a dime. Which is about all it's worth most days. Blasted thing barely works."

"How long have you had it?" I couldn't imagine why the magic in his fanny pack was so weak.

"Goin' on seven years. Got it from the witchy lady. A buddy of mine had brought her out to my place when I was so drunk I could hardly see straight. She unzipped her pouch that was kinda like this one and pulled out all sorts of potions that fixed me right up. After that I was hungry as a baby bear. I kept goin' on about wantin' a big juicy burger. I'll be jigger-swiggered if that woman didn't open her pouch and pull out a giant wad of tinfoil. Inside was the biggest, juiciest darn green chili cheeseburger you've ever laid your eyes on, and it was still hot as blazes. I reckoned it was her bewitched pouch, so I got to thinkin'. If it could deliver up burgers, what couldn't it do?"

"You sure you weren't just seeing things after all that drinking?" asked Violet.

"Nope. It was real, all right. And then I had me an idea that got me feelin' smarter than a tree full of owls. I've always had a hankerin' to win the Texas State Lottery. I figured if I had myself a pouch, it could just as easily cough up the winnin' ticket as it did a burger. I went on down to that hippie place and bought myself one, except the witchy woman wouldn't let me leave with it."

"Why not?" I asked.

"Said she had to charge it up overnight with that piece of froggy amber. Told me to come back the next day. I couldn't hardly sleep a wink, imaginin' what folks would say when ol' Walter Brinker won the Texas State Lottery Million Dollar Grand Prize."

Violet quickly glanced around Walter's dinky trailer. "So, uh no offense, judging by your place here, it looks like that didn't work out so well."

"Cheeky little gal, ain't ya? Well, first day I *did* find myself a genuine Texas Lottery ticket. Scratched off the silver paint with my lucky nickel and won 250 bucks. I couldn't believe my good luck. But the next day I only found me a ten-buck ticket. Day after that it was five. By day three my pouch was empty as a tin cup. It got me wonderin' whether that lady had pulled a fast one. I took the dang thing back three times. Every time she made me leave it overnight so she could charge it up."

Walter shifted in his chair and stared at his boots. "Not that I'm proud of it, but the last time I picked up my pouch, I swiped the amber. Had to or it would have been as useless as a bump on a pickle. Still gotta recharge that thing every dang night. Never again found a 250 buck ticket. In fact, it never coughs up more than five or ten bucks a day, and sometimes it's as empty as a dried up old creek bed. Considerin' I have to drive a hundred miles down to the Texas border to cash 'em in, I wait for the winnin' tickets to pile up before I head down there. Otherwise it would be costin' me too much in gasoline. However, one of these days? I'm gonna unzip this and find the million-dollar big boy."

Looks like Walter had hoped to buy the goose that laid the golden egg and wound up with one that laid the plastic kind instead.

"Mr. Brinker?" I said. "I know the secret to keeping the fanny pack charged for a super long time."

I swear I saw his hands jitter. "Well, spit it out girl."

"I have a friend who has one just like it. It stayed charged for thirty years because mostly she uses it to help other people. Hardly ever for herself. That's what keeps the magic working."

Walter snorted. "Well that won't do me a lick of good. Why would I do somethin' like that? I got nobody to help anyway."

"There's always someone to help," I said.

"Let me get somethin' straight. I invited you anklebiters in here 'cause I thought you could tell me the secret to gettin' my pack to pay off like it should. Now you're speakin' nonsense. What good does it do to help someone else out when *I'm* the one needin' help? Dumbest dang thing I've heard. I think you half-pints best hit the road. You're wastin' my time."

Walter stood and shoved open the front door.

"You don't get it," Violet blurted out. "Madison's Grandma Florida could die if we don't recharge our fanny pack. You *have* to give us the amber."

Walter snapped the door shut and stared at us, scratching his head.

"Florida ain't a grandma any more than I'm a Pinto pony. And she ain't sick. I saw her a couple days back at the Davis-Fleck Drugstore havin' it out in front of everybody with that daughter of hers."

"Uh, not *that* Florida," I lied and stared down at my Keds so Walter wouldn't see my eyes flicking.

"Girl, you're a lousy fibber. Who are you kids anyway?"

Should I level with him? Would it be worth the risk to save my grandmother?

"Look, we can't tell you everything," Noah said just as I was about to spill the beans. "But we need that amber and we'll do almost anything to get it back."

Walter returned to his chair and leaned so close to me I could practically count every pore in his face. "Maybe I don't care who you are just so long as we make a deal. I'll hand over the amber . . ."

"Which you stole in the first place," Violet pointed out.

"Makes no never mind. Like I said, I'll hand it over if you get something for me first. I'm guessin' that if you know Florida, then you know Jack."

As in my Grandpa Jack?

"Years ago Jack Brown and I used to play poker over at Rocky's Lounge. I lost one too many games to him and didn't have the dough to cough up my debt. I was hopin' I could pay him off in homebrew whiskey, except Jack didn't want none of that."

Knowing my grandpa, he probably wanted Walter to live up to his word, fair and square.

"So he made me hand over the key to my storage locker. The scumbucket who owns The Big Lock-Up Storage Shed was one of our poker buddies. He refuses to let me get my stuff until Jack comes off his high horse and gives me back my key. My whole life's in there, or it is if that scoundrel hasn't raked it clean to pay off my debt. So here's the deal. I'll *loan* you the amber if you get that key back from Jack. It's a little silver one with my initials—W.B.—painted on it in red."

Walter glanced over at a clock on the bookshelf.

"Now I'm pretty sure your ten minutes is up. Don't bother showin' your faces again without my key."

And with that he pushed us out the door.

CHAPTER TWENTY-THREE
Hatching a Plan

Since I only had Costa Rican *colones* in my pocket, we couldn't use the pay phone to call Mike. Instead, we walked the two miles back to town, past acres of endless dirt and skittering tumbleweeds. Leroy sniffed every single clump of dry grass like he was a doggie Geiger counter. I figured he must have been hoping for more jackrabbits. I kept thinking about Florida and wondered how she was holding up. Plus, I couldn't get Walter Brinker off my mind. What in the world had made that man so crabby?

"Well, at least he didn't shoot us. That's a plus," Violet said.

"I think he was bluffing," Noah said. "More bark than bite."

"I hope you're right. And that he was telling the truth about loaning us the amber." After what Mike told us about Walter being only fifty percent honest, I didn't trust the guy.

"Any idea how we're going to get that key?" Noah asked.

"I'm thinking," I said.

Violet clutched her stomach. "Yeah, me too. But what I'm thinking about is *dinner*. I'm so hungry I could eat a whale!"

When we walked into Grandma Daisy's kitchen, she'd just finished grilling a tower of cheddar cheese sandwiches on crusty homemade bread. It was as if she'd known we'd be back any second. She set a platter of them on the kitchen table along with a big bowl of cold fruit salad mixed with honey yogurt. We thanked her and eagerly dug in.

"Any luck?" she asked.

"Sort of," I said and then took a giant bite. I wiped a thread of warm cheese from my chin.

Violet chimed in after helping herself to two sandwiches. "Walter Brinker's a dirty stinking rat. He stole the frog amber to keep his fanny pack charged so it would cough up lottery tickets and make him rich."

Grandma Daisy sighed. "The man didn't read the instructions that came with the pouch. That won't work well at all."

"It definitely hasn't." Noah piled a mountain of fruit next to his grilled cheese.

I told Grandma Daisy all about the deal Walter had offered us, and how we had to get the key from Grandpa Jack if we were going to be able to recharge the fanny pack.

She tapped her knobby fingers on the table. "I think Angela could turn out to be a big help. If you don't mind, let me talk to her. We'll have to be delicate about how much we say."

After dinner, Grandma Daisy warmed up one of her famous blueberry pies. It was exactly like the one Rosalie Claire made for us a few days ago, and the same kind my mom used to make before she died. One bite and my head and heart filled with a swirl of happy memories.

"Knock, knock. Guess who?" My mom pushed open the back door and my heart fluttered fast.

"Homework tonight. Thought I'd do it over here." She dropped her backpack on the floor by the kitchen table.

As Grandma Daisy cut her a slice of pie, my mom unzipped the front pocket of her backpack and pulled out a book.

"*The Lion, the Witch and the Wardrobe.* I have to write an essay. Have you read this?" she asked, holding it up.

Only about a zillion times.

"It's my favorite," I said. "The first time my mom read it to me I was five. She loved that book." How freaky did it feel to be telling my kid-mom about her grown-up self?

"Wow, that's crazy! This is my favorite book, too. I'm obsessed. How cool would it be to just walk through a wardrobe into a whole different world?"

"Pretty cool," I said, thinking that a magic TV wasn't too bad either.

My mom took a bite of her pie. "You know what I wish? I wish *I* had a wardrobe like that. Then I'd leave Truth or Consequences and go someplace magical. Once I got to the other side I'd lock the wardrobe door and throw away the key so no one could come find me. Except for you, Daisy. You'd have your own key."

"Thank you, Angela. I appreciate that. And funny you should mention a key." Grandma Daisy joined us at the table, scooting her chair close to my mom.

"You know, Angie, I've always been honest with you and I'm not one for beating around the bush."

My mom stopped chewing and set down her fork.

"The kids came here because they're looking for something important for Rosalie Claire. In order to get it, they need a key your dad may have that once belonged to someone else."

My mom's eyes opened wide. "Did he steal it?"

"No, no. Nothing like that," said Grandma Daisy.

"He won it in a card game," I told her. "It's silver. And has the initials *W.B.* painted on it in red."

She shrugged. "Never seen it."

"Maybe your dad knows where it is. Or your mom," Violet said. "You could ask one of them."

"Yeah? Well, my mother and I aren't exactly on speaking terms right now so that won't be happening. I could hunt around in my dad's dresser sometime when my parents are out."

"The thing is, Angie, you can't just take it. There's a little bit of magic wrapped up in all of this and you know the rule. Your dad has to give it up willingly," Grandma Daisy said.

My mom grinned. "Magic? Ooh, my favorite subject. Tell me more."

Grandma Daisy clasped a hand over one of my mom's. "I wish I could, but this time I just can't. You'll have to trust me."

"I always trust you, Daisy." She sighed and I could tell she wasn't too happy to be left out of the loop.

"So how are we going to get this thing?" Violet's eyes glinted with mischief.

Noah scraped the last bit of pie from his plate. "If you asked your dad, do you think he'd just give it to you?"

"No way. He'd be on to me."

We sat in silence as my brain clicked with schemes. Most were totally dumb, until finally I hit on something that just might work.

"I have the perfect plan. Let's do a scavenger hunt."

CHAPTER TWENTY-FOUR
Scavenger Hunt

"A scavenger hunt? That's genius!" My mom pulled out a piece of blue-striped notebook paper from her backpack and we got to work.

"OK, you can't just ask for the key. That would be too obvious. We need a bunch of stuff on the list so it doesn't look suspicious," she said.

"And a few really strange things that are hard to get. You always need something like that," added Violet.

This was our list:

Green dill pickle with a bite out of it
Red heart-shaped cookie cutter
Purple hairnet
Midnight blue crayon
White toothpaste cap
Yellow rubber band
Orange wind-up toy
Pink sponge
Key with red paint on it
Brown empty toilet paper roll

Noah had suggested that we write a list of things with specific colors so Florida and Grandpa Jack wouldn't think it was odd to ask for a key with red paint.

It was time for Operation Scavenger Hunt. My mom headed home to wait for us to ring the doorbell.

Grandma Daisy handed us an old pillowcase. She'd already dropped in a red heart cookie cutter, a white toothpaste cap, and a brown toilet paper roll. That way it would look as if we'd made progress on our hunt.

We checked them off our list.

"Ready?" asked Violet.

"I guess so." I swallowed hard. My stomach instantly came down with a case of butterflies that felt more like a flock of hyperactive pigeons. Soon I would be face-to-face with my grandparents for the first time since we'd zapped into the past.

"You'll do fine," Grandma Daisy assured us. "Best of luck."

"Thanks, we're going to need it," I said.

Even though we agreed it might be better for Leroy to stay back with Grandma Daisy, he snuck out the door and followed us anyway. I considered taking him back, although Leroy was usually pretty good at sit-stay, except when there was a jackrabbit around. I figured I'd make him wait for us by the front door.

It was weird walking up to the red brick house where my dog and I would both be living so many years in the future. Mostly it looked the same. Even the black iron cowboy cutout was nailed to the garage door, big as life. But Florida's car wasn't parked in the driveway. Maybe it was in the garage since she probably hadn't started filling it up with all of her purchases from the shopping shows. And apparently she'd taken up gardening. Wilted red geraniums were lined up like soldiers against the front wall in a crusty dry flowerbed. Leroy sniffed them and lifted his leg.

"Bet those flowers are happy they're finally getting watered. Maybe they think Leroy's the new garden hose," Violet joked, and we all cracked up.

After Leroy kicked a pile of dirt to cover the wet, I screwed up my courage and rang the bell.

Ding-dong.

"Someone's at the door," I heard Florida shout.

"I'll get it!" yelled my mom.

"Ooh, look who's talking to me now." I could tell that Florida's voice dripped with scorn.

When my mom opened the door, I made my pitch, exactly as I'd rehearsed it.

"Hi! My name is Madison and we're on a scavenger hunt." My voice was super-cheerful and I'm sure it sounded really fake.

We handed my mom the list.

"I bet we have some of this stuff. Come on in." She sounded just as fake as me.

We followed her into the entryway. I told Leroy to sit and stay outside on the front porch. He plopped down on his butt and sat still as a stone.

It was freaky being inside. Even though most of the furniture was different, the house was the same. I had an instant rush of memories. The day I'd arrived after my mom died. How lonely I'd felt. Zapping into the MegaPix for the very first time. It was even odder to think that although they were my memories, none of those things would happen for a long, long time.

When I first spotted Florida, I'm sure I looked as if I'd seen a ghost. She sat on the flowery sofa. Her hair was jet black and HUGE, like she'd jammed her finger in a light socket and her hairdo had exploded in a zillion different directions. Beneath it all she looked just like herself, only younger.

I got a lump in my throat picturing her on her deathbed in Costa Rica. *My friends and I are doing our best to save you,* I thought.

Florida watched TV while my Grandpa Jack sat on an easy chair with his back to us, flipping through the newspaper.

I fought the urge to jump into his lap.

"Ever since we got cable, my mother's been totally into the shopping channels," my mom whispered to me.

"Watch out. Those things can get addicting," I said.

She shrugged. "At least it keeps her out of my hair."

Then I remembered what Rosalie Claire had said about not messing with anything that could change the future. If Florida didn't become addicted to the shopping shows, then we never would have gotten the MegaPix, I wouldn't have met Noah, or met my mom as a kid. And I definitely would not be standing in this spot in the living room, almost twenty years in the past.

When a commercial came on, Florida looked up. "Well, who do we have here?" She plastered on a 500-megawatt smile.

Grandpa Jack glanced at us over his shoulder for just a second and grinned. He still had the same bushy mustache. He went back to reading his paper.

It felt strange that my grandparents didn't know me, but how could they, considering it was way back in 1994 and I hadn't even been born yet? I did my best to pretend I'd never seen them before. I'm sure my smile was as phony as my grandmother's.

"They're on a scavenger hunt," my mom said. "I thought we could help out."

"I suppose we can." Florida smoothed her enormous hair.

That's when Leroy forgot he was supposed to stay by the front door. My mom must not have closed it all the way and he burst into the living room, flinging himself back and forth between Florida and Grandpa Jack, more enthusiastically than when he'd chased the rabbit. His nose twitched and he licked them like they were covered in chicken grease.

Florida screamed. "Get that hairy beast out of my house this instant!"

This was definitely not part of The Plan.

CHAPTER TWENTY-FIVE
Grandpa Jack's Key

Florida gave Leroy a mighty shove off the sofa.

"Go!" she ordered as she brushed his stray white fur from her red polka-dot blouse.

"The dog's only bein' friendly, cupcake." Grandpa Jack chuckled as he wiped a string of Leroy's slime from his cheek. "Maybe you'd best wait in the backyard, little fella." He patted Leroy's head.

"Sorry. I'm so, so sorry. I'll take him out." I had so much apology in my voice that I could see the anger begin to melt from Florida's face.

"Fine." She checked her make-up mirror, examining how much blush my dog had licked clean.

I led him outside. He made himself comfortable on the chaise lounge on the patio. Leroy grinned ear-to-ear, happy to curl up in his favorite napping spot.

When I came back in, Florida was touching up her hair while Grandpa Jack read over our list.

"You." Florida pointed to me after she finished with her hairdo. "Do you know that you and Angela look almost like sisters?"

Gulp.

"Not really," Angela said. "Her eyes are blue and my nose is pointy like Daddy's."

"Tell me Madison, does your mother fuss about your hair? It's straight as a stick. Just like Angela's." Florida sighed as if that might be the worst tragedy in the world.

"My mom likes my hair. It's just like hers."

"See? *Some* mothers like their kids just the way they are," my mom told Florida.

"That's enough, Angela." Florida gave my mom the "knock-it-off-look" I knew so well.

"You kids gettin' excited about Fiesta?" Grandpa Jack asked.

"You bet we are," Violet said.

"Well, you simply can't miss the parade. Angela and I will be wearing the most divine sequined tightrope walker outfits." Florida tossed her head, movie star-style.

"That's what *you* think," my mom said through gritted teeth.

Florida glared at her with a tight smile. "That's what I *know,* Angela Jane. And you have nothing more to say in the matter."

Wow, my mom and Florida sure were nasty to each other.

"So, uh, do you have anything that's on our list?" Violet asked my Grandpa Jack.

"Lemme see. I'm sure Florida's got herself at least a half dozen purple hairnets she can spare. In fact, she probably has some in every color of the rainbow." He stood up to go find one.

"You sit right down, Mr. Jack Brown. I won't have you poking through my things. I'll do it." She bustled toward the bathroom.

"Can I see the list, Daddy?" my mom asked.

"Sure, honeybunch." He handed it over. My mom's eyes flew straight to the bottom of the page.

"Daddy? We might have a key like that, maybe in your top dresser drawer?"

Grandpa Jack stared at my mom. "Angie, how do you know about that key?"

"Actually, I saw it tonight. I was looking for one of my missing socks that I thought might be in your sock drawer."

Wow, she'd found it?! My insides bubbled with happiness.

"I can go grab it," she said.

My grandpa pulled at his black bushy moustache for a long while and then shrugged. "Might as well. It's of no use to me."

While she ran to my grandparents' bedroom, I asked him what the key opened. I was curious about Grandpa's side of Walter's story.

"It's for a storage unit in town," he explained. "That key was a booby prize in a poker game I played way back when Angie was knee-high to a cricket. By now I guess the sorry fella I won it from has given up thinkin' about it. If he ever shows up with the money he owes me, I'm sure my buddy Jerry who owns the place will give the fella a new key."

My mom raced back into the living room, her hand clutched tight.

On her heels was Florida, who must have spent extra time in the bathroom beautifying herself. Her cheeks were streaked pink with fresh blush and her dark hair had been sprayed into a poufy helmet. In one hand she held a purple hairnet. In the other was something pink and sparkly.

"Angela Jane Brown, you tell me this instant why I just found your Fiesta costume at the bottom of the bathroom trash."

My mom ignored her and opened her hand.

"Ta-da!" she said, revealing Walter's key.

Victory!

"Young lady, you answer me when I'm talking to you." Florida's eyes were fiery.

"Please, answer your mother, Angie." Grandpa Jack sounded all worn out.

"You found it there because that's where that hunk of junk belongs. In. The. Trash. I'm not wearing that stupid thing to the parade. We've been over this a million times, *Mother*." She glared at Florida.

"You ungrateful child! Why can't you be like my friends' daughters? We went to a lot of trouble to find these and you're the only one who isn't tickled pink to have the privilege of wearing one."

"Where do you get your information? From the Lying Ladies of the Red Hot Mamas Liars' Club? All the other kids hate it as much as I do. They're just too scared to say so."

"Hit the mute button on your attitude, Angela," Florida snapped.

My mom stared at her feet and squeezed her eyes shut. Was she going to cry?

Florida forced her fakest smile. I know that smile well. I'd seen it so many times before.

"Here's an idea," Florida suggested. "Why don't you model your costume? These kids will tell you how fabulous it looks, won't you, kids? Maybe then you'll see the light."

My whole body squirmed with embarrassment for my poor mom. Violet, Noah, and I traded silent looks.

"I'd rather eat dirt!" My mom began to cry. She ran to her room, the same one that would someday be mine. The door banged shut.

She still had the key.

Florida's cheeks flushed even redder than they'd been from the blush.

Grandpa Jack buried his head in his hands.

"Uh, do you mind if we go get the key?" My voice sounded more like a mouse's than a girl's.

"Suit yourself." Florida sunk into the sofa and turned the TV volume on high.

Violet, Noah, and I hurried down the hallway to my mom's bedroom door. It wouldn't take all of us to get that key, but no one wanted to stay in the same room with my ticked-off grandmother.

I gently knocked.

"Mom," I whispered.

Violet elbowed me in the back.

Uh-oh. Major slip up. I had to think fast.

"Mom . . . uh . . . your *mom* told us we could ask you for the key."
I prayed the door had muffled my mistake.

There was no reply.

"I don't blame you for freaking out." I'd said it loud enough for
her to hear me through the door, but quiet enough so Florida couldn't
make out what I was saying over the blare of her shopping show.

Next thing I knew, the key slid out through the bottom crack of
the door.

"Thanks," I said. "See you tomorrow."

My heart ached for my poor mom. And then, like a strike of lightning, I thought of something brilliant. Could I zap her back to Costa
Rica with me? Then her life wouldn't be so miserable. So what if she
was only fourteen? She was still my mother—or would be someday—
and there was a tie between us that was stronger than the summer sun.
Was that too crazy to consider?

If I brought her back to Costa Rica, would I poof out of existence?
Was it worth taking a chance? Maybe everything would turn out fine
and she could live with Rosalie Claire and Thomas, then I could see her
during my vacations. Or I could move down there and we'd all live
together. When it was time for her to go to college in San Francisco, I'd
get the MegaPix back and play one of the documentary films she made
when she was a student. Then she could just zap back to the time before
she got together with my dad. All I'd have to do is to never, ever let it
slip that she was going to grow up to be my mother. And then I would
still be born.

Even though Rosalie Claire warned us not to tinker with the past
because it might change the future, I figured I might have to make an
exception. I had some thinking to do.

We headed back to the living room. We had to cross in front of
Florida so we could open the sliding glass door to the patio where Leroy
waited on the chaise lounge.

My grandmother's eyes stayed glued to the TV.

"Don't forget the hairnet." Her voice was flat. She tossed the gauzy purple wad on the table.

"Thanks so much, uh, Mrs. Brown," I said.

Violet snatched it and dropped it in the pillowcase. Then we left.

By the skin of our teeth, Plan Scavenger Hunt had worked. And now I tingled with excitement for two reasons. Number one? Maybe I could zap my mom out of there and we'd be together again. And number two? We were getting closer to the magic amber. So close, in fact, that I could almost feel it cupped in the palm of my hand.

CHAPTER TWENTY-SIX
The Mysterious Ring

The next morning, I slipped on my backpack and Mike drove us to Walter's. When we got out of the car, Leroy stayed in the backseat and looked at me with the saddest eyes. My dog has a sixth-sense about these things. He must have figured out he wasn't coming with us, but we couldn't risk making Walter crankier than he already was, and he clearly wasn't fond of Leroy. As Mike drove away, Leroy stuck his head out the open window and yowled. But I wasn't worried. I knew he'd be in safe hands with Mike and Grandma Daisy.

We trudged behind the Shell station toward the doublewide trailer.

"I say we don't let Walter have the key until he hands over the amber. Even swap," Violet said.

Noah and I agreed, and we mounted the steps. I knocked three times on his front door. It creaked open and Walter stared down at us with a scowl.

"Now ain't this a fine howdy-do? I never thought I'd see the likes of you crumb-crunchers again. You have somethin' for me? Or are you stoppin' by to waste my time?"

Something about Walter made me quake in my Keds, although I made myself look him straight in the eye. "We have what you asked for."

"And now we'd like the amber, thank you very much." Violet stuck out her hand.

Walter squinted as if he thought we were pulling a fast one. "Gimme a looksee."

Noah gave a quick nod. "Happy to give you the key, Mr. Brinker, but first we need the amber."

"You young'uns are 'bout as crazy as popcorn on a hot skillet. How do I know it's the right key if I don't take a look at it?"

I guess he did have a point.

"OK, then what if we take the key to the storage place and see if it works?" Noah suggested. "If it opens the lock, you give us the amber."

"Now that's usin' the ol' noggin, boy. Wait here." He shut the door and returned in a split second, jangling a hefty wad of keys and holding the amber, which he dropped into the pocket of his baggy overalls.

"You rugrats can ride in the back of the van. It's just a mile up the road."

He swung open the double doors. The inside was filthy with oily rags and rusty tools. Violet scrambled in.

"We'll meet you there. We're walking. All three of us," I told Walter.

Violet looked at me as if I were nuts.

Stranger danger, I mouthed to her when Walter had his back turned. I wanted to play it safe.

Violet shrugged and crawled out of the van.

"Suit yourself. See ya there." Walter hopped into the driver's seat and took off, leaving behind a cloud of dust.

"What do you think he's got stashed in there that's such a big deal?" Noah asked as we walked up the road.

Violet's eyes glimmered. "I bet he's got stolen jewels. Maybe he robbed a jewelry store."

Given how much he was in love with striking it rich, he could be hiding something like that. Whatever was in there, I had a hunch that inside that storage bin were some of Walter's deepest, darkest secrets.

• • •

The Big Lock-Up Storage Shed was a small cluster of green metal buildings surrounded by a chain link fence and vacant lots. Nothing grew around there except sagebrush and one lonely tree. Walter squatted on the back bumper of his copper van, chewing his nails.

He pointed to number 14B. "Open 'er up," he said.

I slipped the key into the silver metal padlock and twisted. It didn't budge.

"I knew you kids were tryin' to pull a fast one on me."

Uh-oh. What if we hadn't gotten the right key after all?

"Sheesh, don't be such a Negative Nellie," Violet told Walter. "It's an old sticky lock. I saw some of that squirty stuff in the back of your van. Let's try that." She climbed in and returned with a can of WD-40.

"My dad fixed my rusty bike lock with this." She sprayed the lock until it dripped.

"Now try," she said.

I slid the key back into the lock and turned. It clicked and sprung open.

"Told you so." Violet shot Walter a look.

Noah held out his hand. "The amber, Mr. Brinker?"

"Back off skunk-munchers. First I wanna rummage around and see if that scoundrel made off with anything."

"That wasn't the deal," I said. I had a bad feeling about this.

We watched Walter haul out a bunch of junk—scuffed-up tables with broken legs, a red chair with its stuffing oozing from a rip in the seat, and boxes wrinkled from water damage. No stolen jewels in sight.

He pulled out a wooden stick horse with green marble eyes, its mane made from an old string mop.

"Do you think Walter has kids?" Violet whispered to me.

I wondered that too, so I asked him.

"Kids? Nah. This here's old Paw-Paw," Walter told us. "When I was fetched up, we was so poor I had to ride double with my brother on that ol' stick horse. It was a birthday present from my ma."

When he mentioned his mother, his lips pinched into a sad smile. I tried imagining Walter as a little kid, trotting around on that horse. I wondered if he was as bratty then as he was mean now.

When every last scrap had been hauled out into the open, and he'd poked around through some of the boxes, Walter's face turned stony. "Wouldn't you know that son-of-a-badger took the only valuable thing in there? I shoulda known." He kicked the side of his van with the pointy toe of his cowboy boot and left a small dent.

"What are you missing?" I asked.

"Nothin'," he mumbled.

"Can't be nothing or you wouldn't be so cranky," Violet said, pointing out the obvious.

Walter glared at her. "You're a piece of work, little lady. And it's none of your dang business."

"We can help you look for it if we know what it is," I said.

Walter snorted. "It's a little bitty leather box. I needed what was inside to pay off some debts. You wanna look? Knock yourselves out. You ain't gonna find it."

The three of us opened the boxes Walter hadn't checked. We found yellowed newspaper clippings and photos curled at the edges. Noah pried open a metal trunk that had rusted shut on its hinges. Inside was a stack of chipped china dishes, but no small leather box.

I slid open the drawer of a broken down end table. Inside at the very back I spied something.

"Is this it?" I held up a tiny black jewelry box.

Walter's eyes bulged as wide as two desert full moons.

"Gimme that." He stuck out his hand.

Wow. He sure was rude, but I handed it to him anyway. I thought about telling him that saying "thank you" would've been nice, except

Walter looked as if he was about to cry. He opened the lid. A diamond ring shimmered in the sun.

His eyes filled with tears, although he wiped them away with his sleeve before they could escape. In a flash, he bolted to his van and slammed the door.

"Where are you going?" I shouted.

"What about the amber? We had a deal!" Noah raced after the van as it sped from the lot, its tires squealing on the asphalt.

"What a stinking skunk." Violet plunked herself down in the beat-up red chair. "That guy has some serious issues."

Why did he take off like that? Was he too upset about that ring, or did he do it because he never planned to live up to his promise? I didn't have a clue. I did know one thing, though. No way in a million years were we giving up.

CHAPTER TWENTY-SEVEN
Grandma Daisy's Fanny Pack

"Mother of Pearl, who wants to bet that diamond ring was stolen?" Violet said as we shoved Walter's stuff back into the storage unit. "I mean, we already know the guy's a thief."

"Did you see how upset he got when he talked about his mother?" Noah asked. "Maybe the ring belonged to her."

"Or to someone he bumped off with his gun." Violet propped old Paw-Paw in the storage bin and slammed the door.

"You might be jumping to conclusions." Noah bit back a smile.

I had no idea if either one of them was right. At this point *anything* was possible. I snapped the padlock shut and dropped Walter's key into my backpack.

We walked twelve blocks back to town. When we turned onto Broadway, a long banner had been strung across the street. In bright red letters it said: *42nd Annual Fiesta & Parade! Under the Big Top!*

Now that Walter had slipped away with the amber, there was a good chance we'd be staying for Fiesta. At least it gave me more time to make a plan to bring my mom back to Costa Rica.

At the Wildflower, Leroy blissfully chewed on a bone while Grandma Daisy helped a lady pick out healing herbs.

"Success?" she asked us once her customer had paid and left.

I shook my head and we told her everything.

"Personally, I think we should go back to the stinking liar's house right now and *take* the amber, fair and square," Violet said.

I knew better than that. Two wrongs don't make a right. I reminded her that Walter had to give it up willingly for the magic to work.

"Maybe we won't need the amber after all. Look what I got back today!" Grandma Daisy patted a fanny pack strapped around her tiny waist. It was sandy brown like Rosalie Claire's. Stamped into the leather was the image of a white and yellow daisy.

Violet practically jumped up and down. "Now we never have to see that creep-ola Walter again. You can come back to Costa Rica with us and cure Florida!"

An impish smile spread across Grandma Daisy's face. "That's exactly what I was thinking, Violet. And you know what? I've always dreamed about visiting the future."

I wasn't nearly as excited as Violet. "Rosalie Claire's fanny pack still needs to get recharged," I said. *And what about taking my mom back to Costa Rica with me?* I thought because I didn't dare say it out loud.

"Good point, Madison. I have an idea. What if we all zipped or zapped, or whatever you call it, to the future to help Florida? Then we could come back here so you kids can track down the amber. The sooner we see if the magic in my fanny pack is strong enough to set your grandmother on the road to recovery, the better, don't you think?"

Given the way MegaPix-time worked, I knew we hadn't been gone from Costa Rica for even an hour and Florida probably wasn't a whole lot worse. But it was a good idea to see if the magic would be strong enough to cure her. Besides, returning to the future would give me a chance to talk with Rosalie Claire about my plan to bring back my mom.

"Well, what are we waiting for?" Grandma Daisy looked as excited as a kid on the first day of summer vacation.

"OK, let's do it." I fished the remote control out of my backpack.

"Hold your horses. Not yet. Come with me." Grandma Daisy walked double-fast toward the storeroom.

I whistled for Leroy and we all followed Grandma Daisy, pushing past a curtain of colorful beads. The woodsy aroma of musky incense and dried herbs filled my nostrils. The place was three times as big as Florida's living room and crammed with all sorts of things: towers of neatly labeled boxes, a family of old cloth dummies, and ginormous jars of tinctures and dried herbs. Mike was busy pouring dried lavender into a glass container.

"Could you do me a favor and be on customer duty for a spell? The kids and I need a few minutes of privacy."

"You got it." Mike twisted the jar lid shut and headed out through the bead curtain.

"Everybody ready?" I asked once he was gone.

Grandma Daisy rubbed her palms together like she was warming them up for the ride. "My stars, let's get on with it!"

I reached for her small knobby hand and she gripped mine tight. On her other side was Violet, and then Noah. Noah held onto Leroy's collar.

"Ready to go to the future?" I asked.

"Am I ever!" Grandma Daisy grinned.

I pushed the buttons on the remote.

Ping!

I felt the familiar icy cold sparking through my body, but then something peculiar happened. Like a thunderbolt, fiery heat exploded and rushed through my veins. The five of us twisted and turned through a kaleidoscope of swirling colors that quickly turned smoky black as I clung to Grandma Daisy's hand. At first our hands pulsed with electricity, and then the sparks began to fade away.

So did Grandma Daisy. Through her translucent body I saw candy-pink clouds drifting along a turquoise sky. She was dissolving right before my eyes. I could feel her slowly letting go of my hand.

Something was going horribly wrong. We had to go back!

CHAPTER TWENTY-EIGHT
The Rules of Magic

I jammed my thumb on the purple button and the enter button on the remote and watched Grandma Daisy's body return to solid. Once again that familiar icy feeling ran through my veins.

The next thing I knew we were back in the storeroom at the Wildflower. We gasped for breath. Even Leroy sprawled on the floor, panting hard.

"Son of a cheeseball! What just happened?" Violet's eyes searched the room as if she might find the answer hidden up in the rafters.

"No clue," I said. I'd never felt so dog-tired.

"I think I know." Noah's shoulders slumped as he stared at the dusty wood floor.

"Me too." Grandma Daisy's eyes took on a faraway look, like her thoughts were a zillion miles away. "I didn't live to see 2014, did I?"

My voice dissolved into a whisper. "Sorry," I said.

"There's no reason to be sorry, Madison. I should have thought about that. I'd be over one hundred by then for Pete's sake. It makes so much sense. And you know what? It's exciting to understand something more about life and magic."

Her eyes shone like the starry heavens, which seemed kind of strange since she'd just found out she'd be dead. "What we've discovered today is a doozy, kids."

"What's that?" I asked.

"*If something has already happened in the future, it can't be undone.*

You can't travel forward to a time if you've already died. It would undo the dying and the whole order of things. The magic only allows you to go to a time when you already exist, or to the past before you were born."

"You did live a really long time," I assured her, maybe because I felt worse about her dying in the future than she did. "Rosalie Claire said you died in . . ."

Grandma Daisy held up her hand. "Shush, child. That's information no one needs to know. In my book, life still needs a dollop of mystery."

Then it dawned on me. This meant that I wouldn't be able to bring my mom back with me into the future. My chest ached and I bit my bottom lip. I stared off at nothing in particular, listening to the muffled *jingle-jangle-jingle* of Mike ringing up the cash register in the next room.

"What's the matter?" Grandma Daisy's twinkly brown eyes turned soft.

"I shouldn't say." I was pretty sure that my mom dying at such a young age was something else Grandma Daisy would prefer to keep locked up in the vault of future mysteries.

I don't know if she could read my mind, or just my mood, but she got quiet.

"How is Angela? Your mom? In the future, I mean."

Violet and Noah flinched.

Then I couldn't help it. A heavy tear rolled down my cheek. Pretty soon a whole bunch of them fell a mile a minute. For the record, that hadn't happened in a long, long time. I thought my eyes had been all cried out.

Stupid me.

"It was her heart," I said. "A year and a half ago it just stopped. Or a year and a half ago about twenty years in the future."

Grandma Daisy wrapped her arms around me, warm as a blanket.

"Maybe she could go to a doctor now and get fixed, so, you

know . . ." My sobs wouldn't let me finish my words.

Grandma Daisy took my face in her hands and tears streamed down her cheeks too.

"Child, there are just some things you can't undo once they've been done. The time you've lived since your mom passed can't be erased. It's just the way of things."

Deep down I knew she was right. I thought about Rosalie Claire, Noah, Thomas, and Leroy. If my mom hadn't died, none of them would be in my life. And I never would have learned about magic. It didn't make sense that everything that had happened to me in the last year and a half could just poof away.

"My advice? Always keep your mom close to your heart. If your love for her stays strong, she'll live as long as you do."

If that was the case, then I planned to live until I turned at least 103. That way I'd keep my mom alive for practically ever.

"And now you have an extra gift. Not too many kids get a chance to know their mom when she's still a teenager."

Boy, that was the truth. And for that I knew I was lucky.

Violet wiped away her tears and put her arm around me.

Grandma Daisy dug into her fanny pack and found four Kleenexes—one for each of us.

"It's been quite an afternoon. Shall we all go back to my place for a little lemon balm lavender iced tea?"

As tempting as Grandma Daisy's iced tea sounded, I had other things on my mind. When I realized I couldn't take my mom back with me to Costa Rica, it almost felt as if I'd lost her a second time. Then an image of Florida popped into my head, lying in a starched white hospital bed, all hot, sick, and sweaty. She was on the verge of dying. No way was I going to let that happen. It was time to confront Walter, whether he wanted to see us or not.

CHAPTER TWENTY-NINE
The Not-So-Great Stake Out

We begged Mike to drive us out to the old Shell station even though the sky had turned to dusk. When we got there, we watched a pick-up truck peel onto the road. Walter pumped gas into a fancy convertible. It looked as if business had picked up, maybe because of all the tourists coming into town for Fiesta.

"Call if you need me." Mike dropped some coins into my hand and the three of us climbed out of the car. Leroy hung his head, resigned to spend the rest of the day away from me.

We waited until the convertible took off and that's when Walter spotted us. "What do you scum-monkeys want?"

"I think you know," I said. "You made a deal with us."

He spat a wet loogie on the ground.

"Look, Mr. Brinker, a promise is a promise. You said if we gave you the key, you'd loan us the amber. We only need it for one night." I figured that's all it would take to recharge Rosalie Claire's fanny pack. Then the magic would last for another thirty years.

"How do I know you won't run off with it?" He glared at us, all squinty-eyed.

"*Some* people run off with things, Mr. Brinker. Not us," Noah said.

"Besides, you don't want somebody's *death* to be on your conscience, do you?" Violet threw him one of her championship poison dart stares.

Walter stood silent for a moment, like he might actually be considering living up to his word. Then he stuck out his grease-stained hand. "What do you say you gimme your pouch? I'll do the chargin' and you can pick it up in the mornin'."

At first I didn't answer because I had a hunch something wasn't quite right. Noah and Violet shot me quick looks of warning. I could tell we were all thinking the same thing.

Did we have a choice?

Then as if she'd been struck by divine inspiration, Violet's eyes lit up and she whispered in my ear. "Do it. I just came up with a genius idea."

Some of Violet's ideas turned out to be genius, although not always. Like the time she tried to keep her little brother out of her room by stretching a wire along the floor of her bedroom door. He tripped over it, fell, and sprained his wrist. But at least she had one idea when I had zero.

"Do we have ourselves a deal?" Walter folded his arms, waiting for our answer.

"Deal," I finally said, hoping this time Violet had cooked up something brilliant. I unzipped my backpack, hoping everything would turn out OK. When I handed Rosalie Claire's fanny pack to Walter he inspected it, inside and out.

"You ankle-biters come back first thing in the morning. Your pack will be charged up and waiting." He clomped back into the gas station office, taking it with him.

"So what's the plan?" I asked Violet.

"OK, we know the guy is a Lying Luigi, right? So we wait here all night and keep a lookout in case he tries to take off with the fanny pack."

"What if he does? Are we going to run fifty miles an hour behind his van?" asked Noah.

"I don't know. We could call 9-1-1 from the phone booth, right?"

That was Violet's plan? To stay here all night? By *ourselves*? OK, it's not like I was scared, except it seemed kind of risky and not exactly "genius." After all, Walter had a getaway car and a gun. We had a few quarters and my nearly empty backpack.

"Look guys, I've thought it all out. Or most of it. We'll take turns on lookout duty. It'll be just like camping out."

That was the magic word Noah needed to hear. *Camping.* "I'm in," he said.

Since Noah and his dad used to camp every summer before they bought their house, he was an expert. "We'll find a place where he can't see us, but we can still keep an eye on him."

It was two against one. What could I do? Besides, I didn't exactly have a better idea. "I'll let Grandma Daisy know we won't be back tonight."

I called her from the pay phone. She fretted that we hadn't eaten dinner so I assured her we'd be A-OK. She told me to stay safe and to call her or Mike if we needed anything at all.

We stayed out of sight until dark when Walter put up the closed sign and went back to his trailer. The night had turned inky black, lit only by the stars and a sliver moon. Noah went searching for something to use as a shelter.

Violet and I were getting hungry. I checked my backpack and found zero-zippo-zilch. Not even a packet of Monkey Poop. Our stomachs growled in unison. It was going to be a long night.

When Noah returned with a sheet of plywood he'd found near an abandoned ramshackle shed next door, we propped it at an angle against the gas station's side wall to make a cozy lean-to. Then we crawled in and craned out our necks. We had a pretty good angle on Walter's place. The blue flicker of his TV lit up his bedroom window.

"After his lights go out, we'll take turns keeping an eye on that two-faced worm. One hour shifts. Then we can also take turns getting some sleep." Violet yawned and her stomach made gurgly noises.

"Too bad we didn't bring food," Noah said.

"I'm *starving*," Violet groaned. "By morning we could all be a pile of bones."

We listened to the night sounds and played a game, trying to distract ourselves from our growling bellies. We counted up all the notes in the symphony of coyote yips and cricket chirps. When we'd tallied 213, we heard a different sound. Car tires rolling along the pavement.

"Is Walter leaving?" Noah asked. We peeked out from our lean-to. The copper van was still parked outside and the TV blazed blue through the window.

Headlights lit up the gas station as bright as sunrise. We scooted back undercover and held our breath.

"Maybe someone stopped for gas," I whispered.

"Or maybe Walter has an accomplice and they're going to steal the fanny pack together," Violet said.

The car door clicked open and shut. We heard the *crunch, crunch, crunch* of boots, circling the gas station. The sound edged closer.

"Ingenious hiding place, kids!" Mike grinned. "I hope you're hungry." He held up a big woven picnic basket. "Courtesy of Grandma Daisy."

"Tell Grandma Daisy she's my favorite person in the entire universe." Violet grabbed the basket.

"What am I? Burnt toast?" Mike's bottom lip stuck out in a jokey pout.

"You're *both* our favorites," I said, and he winked.

After Mike left, we dug into our midnight picnic under the shelter of our plywood hiding place. Grandma Daisy had packed turkey and avocado sandwiches, a thermos of lavender lemonade, and a whole blueberry pie. We stuffed ourselves silly, eating every last crumb. The three of us stretched out for a quick rest, waiting for our stomachaches to go away, our yawns to quit, and for Walter's lights to switch off for the night.

Noah fell asleep before we could decide on our shifts, so I took the first one. Violet stayed awake to keep me company and caught me up on everyone we knew on Bainbridge Island. Whiny Molly Cooper was dating some fourteen-year-old guy who'd just moved to the island from Seattle, which I thought was super weird since she was only twelve. Our friend Mikayla Jackson had won the Washington State Middle School Inventor's Fair by making a butter spreader out of an empty glue stick container crammed with butter. I wasn't at all surprised since Mikayla was way more clever than your average genius. And for the third year in a row, Pavel Dhailwal scored the winning goal in the Island Cup soccer tournament. Even though I'd made new friends in Truth or Consequences, I still missed my old ones. Hearing about everyone almost helped me feel as if I'd never left.

The last time I checked Walter's, I was so sleepy that I wished I'd brought Scotch tape to stick my eyelids open. I nudged Violet and told her it was her turn to take over, although I can't remember if she heard me.

The next thing I knew, the morning light rushed into our lean-to. The coyote yips and cricket chirps had been replaced by the coos of mourning doves. Both Noah and Violet were curled into balls, fast asleep like a couple of puppies. I glanced over at Walter's trailer. His copper van was gone.

CHAPTER THIRTY
Missing

"We are so lame!" Violet clapped her hand over her mouth to cover her yawn after I nudged her awake. "I swear we only closed our eyes for a second."

"It's my fault," I confessed. "I should have made sure you were up before I fell asleep."

Noah groaned and held his stomach. "And I shouldn't have fallen asleep before we figured out our shifts. Blame it on a sugar coma. Too. Much. Pie."

"There's no such thing." Violet reached for the empty pie tin. She ran her finger over a tiny blob of leftover blueberry goo, and popped it in her mouth. Then she peeked out of the lean-to.

"I have an idea. Come on, guys." She wriggled from the shelter and headed straight toward Walter's trailer.

"I'm pretty sure he's not home," I said, but we followed her anyway.

"Who cares? Maybe he left the fanny pack inside." She climbed the front steps and reached for the door handle.

My stomach tightened into a fat knot. And while I didn't want to stomp on Violet's idea, at least I had to tell her what I was thinking. "Breaking in is a big deal, you know."

"Not to mention against the law," Noah added.

"Technically it isn't breaking in. It turns out Walter didn't lock his door." She pushed it wide open.

Tell that to the police, right?

"What if he just ran out to get something and he'll be right back? We could get caught," I said.

"Madison, don't be a chicken, OK?" Violet disappeared inside.

I turned super sweaty from my forehead to my toes. My heart raced. I should have told her to stop right then and there because I knew what we were doing was dead wrong. I just couldn't bring myself to put my foot down. Not to my best friend. Maybe I really *was* a chicken.

Noah followed her. I gave in and walked through the door.

"Let's do this fast, please," I whispered, even though no one was around to hear but us.

My eyes darted around the room and landed on the kitchen table. In the center was the old black-and-white photo of the prom couple. It had been pulled from its frame and its edges were cracked and dirty. I flipped it over. On the back, written in loopy blue ink, it said *Walter and Betty*. It was *Walter* in the picture? He looked so young and happy.

"Check this out," I said.

Violet picked up the picture and stared. "Whoa. Do you think Betty was Walter's wife?"

"What do you think happened to her?" Noah asked, and I wondered the same thing too.

Violet put the picture back, and we searched every nook and cranny in Walter's house as I tried to ignore my stomach knot. Finally, Violet declared that we'd come up empty. The pouch was officially gone.

Now what?

That's when we heard the distant ding of someone pulling into the gas station. I froze.

"What if it's Walter? Let's get out of here." Noah scurried to the front door.

"No, the back way," I said. "If he drives up front, we don't want him to see us coming out of his house." Noah gave me the thumbs up and I started for the rear screen door.

We slipped outside and crept around to the front of the trailer.

But the van was still missing in action. Over at the gas station, Mike was waiting for us by his car. We ran over to greet him.

"I had a feeling you kids might need a ride." He opened the passenger door and gave a royal bow. "Your carriage awaits."

"Maybe we shouldn't leave yet," said Violet. "We have a little unfinished business."

"I don't think Walter will be back any time soon," I said. I have no idea how I knew that, except I could feel it in every pore of my body. I slid into the car while Noah ran back to retrieve the picnic basket.

On the drive back, Violet, Noah, and I sat in silence.

"Rough night?" Mike finally asked.

"You can say that again. Not only is Walter a liar fifty percent of the time, he's a hundred percent double-dealing rat," Violet said. "He stole the fanny pack."

Mike let out a low whistle. "And right from under your noses? Boy, that stinks."

"We messed up and fell asleep," I admitted.

"Ouch. But you know, the guy has to make it into town sometime or another. Nobody stays hidden for long around here. You'll find him."

Mike dropped us off at Grandma Daisy's. "Gotta open up the shop. With Fiesta tomorrow, the Wildflower's going to be a mob scene."

When we walked in, Leroy practically bowled me over with kisses. His tail wagged so fast it became a blur. He trotted behind us to the kitchen, where Grandma Daisy scrambled eggs with Hatch green chiles, a spicy New Mexican delicacy.

"Welcome back. Is everybody hungry?" She ladled the eggs onto four plates.

"I'm still full from last night." Noah groaned.

"Thanks for sending the picnic," I said.

Noah and I picked at the eggs. Violet managed to wolf down half of hers before stopping.

None of us said a word. We didn't have to. All Grandma Daisy had to do was take a good look at our faces.

"Oh dear. I'm afraid to ask how it went."

We confessed we'd fallen asleep on the job.

"A rookie mistake," admitted Noah.

"I could kick myself," I said. "I really messed up."

"I guess that makes us the Mighty Trio of Idiots," Violet added.

"Don't be so hard on yourselves. Everyone makes mistakes. And you know why?" Grandma Daisy asked.

"Because they're really, really stupid like us?" Violet took another bite of her eggs.

Grandma Daisy patted Violet's hand. "No, it's because we're all really, really *human*. And if anyone here thinks they'll never make another mistake, raise your hand."

We all sat there—Grandma Daisy, Violet, Noah, and me—our hands resting on the table. Not even Leroy raised a paw, because sometimes I think he believes he's human, too.

Grandma Daisy drummed her fingers on the kitchen table. "Now, what are we going to do about Walter Brinker?"

We didn't have a second to think about it. We were interrupted by a sharp banging on the back screen door. It was Florida, mad enough to spit nails.

"Daisy." Florida's voice sounded bitter cold.

"Good morning, Florida. Is something wrong?" She ignored my grandmother's nasty tone.

"Yes, something is wrong. Angela has run away. The school just called to say she didn't show up this morning. Would you know anything about that?"

"Oh dear, I don't. How terribly upsetting." Grandma Daisy's eyes clouded with worry.

Then Florida glared at Violet, Noah, and me. "Well, well. It looks like you three are playing hooky too. Is it possible *you* had something to do with this?"

"Uh, no, Mrs. Brown," I squeaked.

"Honestly, not at all," said Noah.

"If I discover you're lying, I'll have no problem tracking down your parents and giving them a piece of my mind."

Good luck with that, I thought.

Violet kicked me under the table and we shared a look, which Florida saw. Her face screwed up in a sneer.

For a split-second I questioned why we were even bothering to help my grandmother. Although I knew that in the long run, Florida-of-the-future would learn how to be a little bit nicer.

"What if something bad happened to her?" Noah asked.

I knew that wherever my mother was, she was safe. If something really terrible had happened, she would have told me about it back when we lived on Bainbridge Island. My guess? She'd run away because she and Florida had a fight.

"Oh please. I doubt it. She's probably sulking somewhere after picking a silly little battle with me this morning."

See? Just as I thought.

"We can help you look for her," I offered.

"Yep. Just call us *CSI: Truth or Consequences*," Violet said.

"Excuse me? CSI?" Florida's forehead scrunched up in confusion.

Uh-oh. The detective show, *CSI*, wouldn't be on television for years.

"She only means we'll be great sleuths," Noah said.

"Do whatever you please. If you find her, make sure you tell her she's going to be in a load of trouble when she gets home."

With that, Florida slammed the door and stomped back down the steps.

Great. Walter had disappeared with the fanny pack. My mom was missing. And Florida was still lying on her deathbed in the future. I longed to talk to Rosalie Claire and ask her what to do, but I knew we were on our own.

"I'm going to look for my mom," I said.

"We're coming with you," said Violet.

CHAPTER THIRTY-ONE
Searching for Mom

OK, here's the thing. I really wanted to look for my mom by myself because I wanted to find her by myself. I longed to spend time with her with no one else around. Just my kid-mom and me. Except I didn't want to make my friends mad since I knew how badly they wanted to help. Besides, we might have an easier time finding her if everyone searched. Then we could get back to tracking down Walter Brinker.

We left Leroy at the house. I loved my dog, but I didn't want to have to worry about keeping an eye on him. Before we left, Grandma Daisy unzipped her newly mended fanny pack and pulled out a doggie bag. Leroy grinned, snatched it in his jaws, and trotted with it into the kitchen.

"T-Bone steak. Cooked rare. The fastest way to a dog's heart," she said.

The four of us left the house and took off on foot.

"Maybe while we're looking for your mom we'll find Walter Brinker, too," said Violet. "Two birds with one stone."

"That, my dear, would be a gift from the gods." Grandma Daisy drew her hands together, palm to palm, as if in prayer.

We all agreed to head to the park. Grandma Daisy said it was the place my mom loved most. As we wound our way through town, Fiesta workers taped signs in shop windows and storeowners swept off sidewalks that would eventually be littered with confetti, empty soda cups, and balled-up napkins soaked with ketchup.

Ralph Edwards Park bubbled with even more activity. The building of all the carnival games and food booths had begun.

"Yum. Barbecue . . . cotton candy . . . tacos . . . funnel cakes . . . *chili dogs*. I live for this stuff. Tomorrow's going to be a good day." Violet licked her lips over the promise of all the junk food as the signs were nailed up one by one.

It sure wasn't going to be a good day if my mom was still missing and we didn't find Rosalie Claire's fanny pack.

We followed Grandma Daisy to the pond where Rosalie Claire would teach me to fish nearly twenty years in the future. We also kept a lookout for Walter. Two older men stood on the bank, casting their lines into the water, and a mother chased her toddler, making sure she didn't fall in.

My mom wasn't there. Neither was Walter Brinker.

Grandma Daisy thought we should check down by the Rio Grande. We walked by two boys kicking a soccer ball past their friend who sat moping on the sidelines.

"Don't be such a baby," one of the boys shouted to the grumpy kid.

And that's when I knew for a fact that my mom wasn't down by the river.

I flashed back to when I was seven. I'd lost a soccer tournament I'd been sure my team would win. My frustration and sadness had rolled themselves into one giant ugly ball that sat like a lump in my belly. I wasn't usually a temper tantrum kind of kid, but that day I blew it. I was like a hurricane. A tornado. A tropical typhoon.

That night when my mom put me to bed, she told me what she did when she was a kid and needed to cool off. She'd climb a wooden ladder, counting all twelve rungs one-by-one as she went. She'd push open a trapdoor in the ceiling and hoist herself into a dusty attic. Then she'd sit up there and think for as long as it took until she was ready to face the world.

The next morning, my mom had helped me make my own place in the attic of our house on Bainbridge Island. We hauled up a threadbare velvet chair we'd bought at Goodwill, and my old baby blanket. We set them in a corner near a small round window with a perfect view of our Japanese maple tree that had turned fiery orange that fall. We named it my "thinking corner." I rarely went up there, although it was a comfort to know that I could.

And it's where, after my mom died, I spent almost four days straight. Violet's mom had stayed at our house to take care of me and she'd run food up to the attic that I barely ate. I only decided to come down because of Violet. She crawled up there on the morning of the fourth day. "You're my best friend and I'm staying with you until you're ready to come down," she'd said. We played Crazy Eights till sunset, and then together we climbed down the ladder.

Where was my mom's attic? There wasn't one at Florida's house on Grape Street, or at Grandma Daisy's.

The four of us scrambled down to the river, but the image of my mom hiding in an attic crowded out every other thought from my head.

"Hey guys. Why don't you look around here? I need to go check out another place."

"Where?" asked Violet.

I had a feeling, although I didn't want to say. "It's probably nothing. Just a hunch."

"Never underestimate hunches," Grandma Daisy said.

"I'll meet you back here in, I don't know, like half an hour?"

"I hope you find her." Noah gave a hopeful smile.

"I'll come with you," said Violet.

Don't get me wrong. Violet is my best friend. She's been with me through thick and thin. But this was something I knew I had to do by myself.

"We need to talk. In private," I whispered in her ear.

Violet looked puzzled. She followed me back up the riverbank to the seesaw on the kiddie playground.

My mouth turned dusty dry. I hated saying anything that might hurt her feelings or make her mad. Besides, I knew exactly what Violet would do if she were in my situation. She'd have the guts to stand up for herself. She'd tell me the truth. I swore to myself that this time I wouldn't chicken out. It was my turn to tell my best friend exactly what I needed.

"I have to do this alone," I said.

"You're kidding, right?" Violet gave me the dreaded eye-roll. "We do *everything* together. I'm coming with you."

"Not this time."

"You can't stop me. It's a free country."

I looked away and said nothing. I felt another knot growing in my gut.

"Seriously, Madison? I thought we were best friends."

"I never said we weren't," I mumbled and wished it were easier to stand up to her.

Then I turned and ran away. If I knew Violet, which I really did, I'd bet a bazillion bucks she stood there watching me with dagger darts blasting from her eyes.

I sprinted along Riverside Drive, wishing I'd been able to tell her exactly why I needed to do this. On Main Street I jogged past swarms of tourists, straight to the Wildflower Mercantile. I caught my breath and pushed open the door.

CHAPTER THIRTY-TWO
The Attic

Inside the Wildflower, dozens of customers filled their shopping baskets to the brim like it was the last store on earth. There was a growing line at the cash register, and Mike was a nervous wreck. I walked in just as a lady in a long, Indian print skirt and a brightly colored babushka handed him her pile of purchases.

"My prayers have been answered! Madison, I need a favor. We're out of paper. Could you run in the back and grab a pile and wrap up these crystal balls?"

What could I say? Mike needed my help. I pushed past the colorful curtain of beads into the storeroom. Because of the clutter, I had to poke around until I finally found a stash of yellowing newspapers.

Then I saw something I hadn't noticed before. In the far corner, a wooden ladder reached high up to a trapdoor in the ceiling. My whole body tingled with certainty. That had to be my mom's attic.

I hurried back with an armload of newspapers and dumped them on the counter.

"Wow, where'd you dig up these relics? We have plain white wrapping paper back there somewhere."

"Sorry. It's all I could find."

"No worries. Let's use it up. Can you give me a hand for a quick second or two?"

I desperately wanted to race up that ladder, but I didn't feel right about bailing on Mike. Besides, would it really be the end of the world if I put off looking for my mom for a couple of seconds?

I carefully wrapped the first crystal ball in thick layers of newspapers that were almost old enough to be antiques.

"Ronald Reagan Sworn in as 40th President," read the headline. And playing at the El Cortez theater was a movie I'd actually watched a couple of years ago on video with Violet, *The Empire Strikes Back*. That's when we both became obsessed with Yoda and talked like him for two months straight.

Wrap up the second crystal ball I will, I thought in Yoda speak.

I reached for more newspaper and something in *The Sierra County Sentinel* caught my eye. The prom picture from Walter's house.

Under the photo it said: "Elena and Roberto Montoya proudly announce the engagement of their daughter, Betty, to her high school sweetheart and Hot Springs High School star-quarterback, Walter Brinker."

What the heck? They'd been engaged? Did they ever get married? Were they divorced, or did Betty die? Could that have been her engagement ring in the little leather box?

I carefully tore out the article, folded it over, and slid it into my jeans pocket.

When Mike handed me another customer's handful of treasures to wrap, I knew I had to come clean.

"Mike, I'm so sorry. I'd like to keep helping, but I can't. My, uh, Angela is missing. I think she might be up in the attic."

"Well, why didn't you say so, Madison? No worries. I can take it from here."

I thanked Mike and pushed my way back through the beaded curtain. I ran to the ladder and began to climb, counting the rungs one-by-one.

One. Two. Three. I could feel my face flush and my forehead get sweaty.

Four. Five. Six. Was I afraid of not finding her?

Seven. Eight. Nine. Or was I more afraid that if I did find her I wouldn't know what to say?

Ten. Eleven. Twelve.

I reached up and popped open the trapdoor.

CHAPTER THIRTY-THREE
Finding Mom

Through the crack of the lifted trapdoor I saw the light of a single bare bulb hanging from the ceiling. My mom sat cross-legged on the floor beneath it, reading *The Lion, the Witch and the Wardrobe.* The rest of the room was empty, just wide-planked wooden floors covered with a thick coat of dust.

I hoisted myself up through the opening. Startled, she sprang to her feet, banging her head on the low wood ceiling.

"Ow!" she moaned, rubbing away the sting. "You scared the bejesus out of me. How did you know I was up here?"

I shrugged. "A good guess?"

"Well, if my mother talked you into finding me, then I'd appreciate it if you don't tell her where I am."

"Never in a zillion years," I promised.

My mom eyed me in a curious way, as if she was trying to figure me out. Then she settled back onto the floor and held up her book.

"It's the third time I've read this. Unfortunately, this attic is the closest thing I'll ever have to my own magic cupboard. It's the farthest place I can go to escape my mother and this boring old town. Which is *so* pathetic."

"You won't live in Truth or Consequences forever."

My mom gave me a look like I was half-crazy.

"What are you, a fortune teller or something?"

Oops, maybe I should have said that she didn't *have* to live here forever. I needed to be more careful.

"In a few years, you could move anywhere." Except with me down to Costa Rica. I squeezed the thought from my mind so I wouldn't turn into a crybaby.

"Easy for you to say. If I'm lucky, maybe I'll get to go to college up in Albuquerque. The problem is, most people who grow up here never leave. Everybody just hangs around and dries out in the desert. It's like a town filled with dead carcasses. Except for Rosalie Claire. She got away."

"You could be like her. Go someplace new. Start over."

"I don't know." She twisted a strand of her stick-straight, nut-brown hair that looked so much like mine.

But I knew. She *had* to leave. If she stayed here forever, I wouldn't be born.

"Have you ever thought about moving to, say, San Francisco?" I knew that's exactly where my mom had lived for six years, and it was the city where I'd been born.

"Never. That would be like living in some alternate universe. People like me don't get to do that kind of thing."

Wow. It broke my heart to see my mom be so hard on herself. To have so little hope and imagination for the future.

"What would I even do there? I mean, other than finally getting to breathe because I'd be far enough away from mother."

It was weird to hear my mom talk that way about Florida, although I understood. She'd had fourteen years of her mother trying to make her into someone she wasn't. I'd only had a year and a half of it. And except for when she started to get sick a few months back, Florida had mellowed some.

But I knew exactly what my mom could do because she'd already done it. In the future, that is.

"Well, uh, since you like to make videos, you could go to college for that. Someone's mom I know went to film school at San Francisco

State. Afterward, she got a job making documentaries. She loved it."

Of course that "someone" I knew was me, and my mom had been a filmmaker until a few years after I was born. Was I directing her future? What if I'd said nothing? How would she have known to move to San Francisco after high school? Did I make that happen or was I just making it easier for her to follow her destiny?

"Wow. San Francisco. That would be awesome beyond words." Her eyes lit up with the possibilities.

But she quickly dropped her head in her hands. "Until then I'm stuck with My-Mother-the-Dictator."

"At least it's only four more years."

"Four years of torture." She wiped away a stray tear that had escaped down her cheek.

"Want my opinion?" I asked.

"Why not?" she sighed.

"Sometimes it's easier to give in on some of the small stuff so you can keep the peace. Be the stronger person."

It's what my mom had taught me, so I was just returning the advice.

"You sound like my dad. He always says that."

I shrugged. "He might be right."

"Not this time. Do you know why I ran off? My mother is not only insisting that I ride on their float wearing that gross pink monstrosity, she made a big glittery sign she wants me to hold that says, *Hot Pink Chicky Boom-Booms*. How humiliating is that? Everyone I know is going to be watching the parade."

"OK, that's pretty bad," I admitted.

"You see? I just can't do it. I'm not the "chicky" girly-girl she wants me to be."

"What if you made a deal with her? Tell her you'll wear the costume if you don't have to carry the sign. And, I don't know, maybe pull some shorts over the bottom of the costume. Tell her you need to do it your way, but you still really want to ride in the parade with her."

"No way, because I really don't. That would be lying." Even at fourteen my mom was reminding me to tell the truth.

"I guess you're right. Then just say you know it's important to her and that's why you're willing to do it. Or part of it, anyway."

"I suppose I could do that. Ugh! I can't believe I'm going to give in!"

"Nah. Don't look at it that way. You're just keeping the peace. Then after the parade, you can put a t-shirt over that gross pink sparkly thing, shoot your video, and hang out with your friends."

"How did you get to be so smart? What are you, like, eleven?"

"I turned twelve in April," I said. "I don't know. I guess I learned a lot from my mom."

"You're so lucky. Your mom must be amazing."

"She is. The best in the world."

My mother looked straight into my eyes. It felt odd because even though she was only fourteen, they were still her eyes, gold flecks on brown. The ones that had always beamed straight into my heart every time she'd tuck me in at night and every time she'd told me that she loved me.

"OK, this may sound ultra-strange. I met you like, what? Three days ago? But it's as if I've known you forever. Like we're sisters or something. And one thing my mom might be right about is that we almost do look as if we *could* be sisters. Weird, don't you think?"

"Yeah, super weird. I feel like I've known you forever too." My heart raced so fast I thought it might burst from my chest. If only I could tell her who I really was.

"Madison, you're one of the most amazing people I've ever met. You, Grandma Daisy, and Rosalie Claire."

It made me happy to be in such good company.

"You know, I love the name Madison. If I have a kid someday, maybe I'll name her that. Then if I'm lucky, she'll turn out to be as awesome as you."

"Thanks. Maybe she will," I said.

We heard the shuffling of footsteps below.

"Madison? Angela?" It was Grandma Daisy.

"Time to go face the rest of my life." My mom took a deep breath. "Thank you."

Then she hugged me. I wanted to stay wrapped in her embrace forever, my mom's heart beating so close to mine. Finally, she pulled away and smiled. Then together we lifted the trapdoor and, rung by rung, climbed down the ladder.

CHAPTER THIRTY-FOUR
Violet

"Look who you found, Madison! Angie, you worried the daylights out of me." Grandma Daisy opened her arms.

"Sorry, Daisy," my mom said as they hugged.

"Well done." Noah's mouth curved in a crooked smile. "When you didn't come back, we *thought* you might be here."

Violet didn't say anything. Her lips were closed tight and she wouldn't even look at me.

We went back out into the store. It still swarmed with tourists. Grandma Daisy pushed up her sleeves and got to work, helping customers choose herbs from jars.

"Ooh, Madison, check it out!" My mom peered through one of the glass-topped counters.

She pointed to a pair of iridescent white beaded moonstone bracelets, speckled with electric blue. Beside them a handwritten card said: "Moonstones bring the wearer what they really need in life. These stones symbolize new beginnings."

"We totally need these bracelets. Or at least I do. And if we each have one, we can always remember each other."

"Wow, they're beautiful!" I wished I could tell her why I'd remember her always even if we didn't have matching bracelets. But still, the thought of having one made my heart sing. "They're kind of expensive. Twenty-five dollars each." Besides, I only had Costa Rican *colones* and a few quarters left over from Mike.

My mom dug twenty dollars out of her jeans pocket and smiled. "Daisy always gives me a discount."

Grandma Daisy pulled the bracelets from the display case. "You girls couldn't have made a better choice. Although I'm not surprised. This is also the stone of intuition."

Grandma Daisy took the twenty-dollar bill and called it even. We rolled the moonstone bracelets onto our wrists and compared them side-by-side.

"Hey, now we really match. And you have almost as many freckles on your arm as I do," my mom said.

"Yep, enough to play connect-the-dots."

She giggled. "Good one. I'll have to try that sometime."

"Thank you. I love my new bracelet," I said, and then I hugged her again.

Mike must have put Noah to work because he was busy wrapping up purchases. But Violet? The whole time she'd been standing by herself at the far end of the counter. It bugged me that was she still angry. She didn't get mad at me often, probably because I almost always let her have her way. This time I knew I'd absolutely positively made the right choice. Although maybe I didn't exactly handle it in the best way. I owed her an apology.

I told my mom I'd be right back.

"Violet, we need to talk," I said.

She turned away and stared down into the display case.

"I'm sorry," I told her. "Sometimes when you only want to do things your way it's kind of frustrating. I had to do this by myself so I could spend time alone with my mom. I didn't want to hurt your feelings, and I shouldn't have run away from you like that. I was rude. I apologize."

Violet traced her finger along the edge of the glass counter. "No, I'm the one who should be sorry. I was being a brat," she confessed. "I just get really excited sometimes and maybe I don't always think stuff through. And you're right. I guess I do want to do things my way a lot. Of course you needed to spend time alone with her. Holy schnikies, she's your *mom*."

"It's OK," I said. "We're still best friends, right?"

"Always and forever. You had a hunch where to find her, didn't you, Madison?"

I nodded.

"That's so cool. It seems like that's the kind of magic you're pretty good at."

Were hunches a kind of magic too? She might be right about that. I threw my arms around her. I knew right then I would never have a better friend than Violet.

When Noah finished wrapping up amulets, stones, and crystal balls, we told Grandma Daisy we were going to continue our search for Walter Brinker. I was itching to get the pouch back, safe and sound.

"Still looking for whatever it is you need for Rosalie Claire?" my mom asked.

"Unfortunately, yes," I told her.

My mom offered to come with me. I wanted nothing more than to spend every spare second I could with her, although if we found Walter when my mom was with us, there would be too much explaining to do.

"I wish you could, but like Grandma Daisy said, it has to do with some magic stuff we can't talk about. Sorry."

"No biggie. Really. I should go home and face my mother. You're coming to the parade tomorrow, right? I mean *everybody* in town will be there. Including me, if I'm not grounded."

"You better not be grounded because we plan to cheer you on in your spangly suit."

My mom groaned. Then she caught my eye and smiled.

Violet, Noah, and I left the Wildflower and we walked through town, two miles to the Shell station. There was no sign of Walter or his copper van.

"Walter Brinker scores one. The Mighty Trio? Zero," Violet sighed.

"We're not giving up," Noah said. "And we're not letting him win this thing."

"Remember when my mom said everyone in town shows up for Fiesta? If that's true, maybe Walter will be there too."

"Let's cross our fingers on that one," Violet said.

Then the three of us did exactly that.

CHAPTER THIRTY-FIVE
Walter Brinker

It was parade day. We grabbed our backpacks and headed into town. My moonstone bracelet glinted in the morning sun. The sky was blue, and white puffy clouds floated overhead. Leroy trotted along on his rope leash, happy to be part of our pack again. He grinned and his tail wagged at warp speed.

The whole time we kept an eagle-eye lookout for Walter. Today *had* to be the day we'd find him. I could practically feel it in the air.

We'd made a plan to meet Grandma Daisy after the parade at the Wildflower where she and Mike were working all day selling trinkets and treasures to the tourists.

Alongside us, crowds of people hustled into town carting folding chairs and coolers. Parents trailed behind their kids who bounced up and down at the promise of cotton candy and carnival games.

When we turned the corner onto Broadway, Noah nudged me. "Look who's doing his grocery shopping."

Walter's copper-colored van was parked in front of the Bullock's Shur-Sav.

"I'll wait outside with Leroy," Noah offered. "Hurry before he gets away!"

Double-speed, Violet and I dashed into the market.

Walter stood in the checkout line with a small basket of groceries. Strapped around his waist was his black fanny pack.

Where was Rosalie Claire's?

I ignored my jitters and cleared the nervousness from my throat.

"Going to the parade?" I asked.

Walter froze.

"The parade?" I repeated. "Are you going?"

When he snapped out of his spell, he looked at anything and everything except for us. "Nope. I'm gettin' as far away from this brouhaha as I can."

"Before you leave, you owe us something," I told him.

"What's that?" he asked, pretending to be all innocent.

"Don't play dumb." Violet stared at him without a blink.

"Here's the deal, rugrats. I recharged your pack and at first it just coughed up a big ol' wad of lint. Next I found an old shoelace. But this morning there was a twenty-five-buck winning ticket. How 'bout I keep it just a few more days? I could use the dough."

"I need it for my grandmother *now*. That fanny pack will wear out just the way yours did, because, like I told you, it works best when you use it to help other people. Why won't you believe me?" I stared him straight in the eye, same as Violet.

We were interrupted by a commotion at the checkout counter. A lady with a baby in a carrier on her back had a plastic shopping basket filled with milk and baby food. The checker told her that her debit card didn't work because there wasn't enough money in her bank account.

"I'm sorry. I have a little cash, but I'm short twenty dollars," she told the clerk. Her voice was panicky.

"Excuse me." I reached over and tapped her on the shoulder. "This man can help you."

I pointed to Walter.

Walter looked at me as if I were a three-headed alien.

"Oh, could you, sir? I'd be so thankful. It's been a hard month. I'll repay you. Honest." Her eyes brimmed with tears.

"I have no idea what this little gal is talkin' about," he said, meaning me.

"Unzip your pouch, Walter. You might have twenty dollars in there." I crossed my fingers I was right.

"You know I only got lottery tickets."

"Then prove it," Violet said.

Walter grumbled and yanked open the zipper.

His look of surprise could have made the angels sing. Even if he tried, I don't think he could have stopped the grin from spreading across his face.

Walter pulled out a brand-spanking new twenty-dollar bill.

"Well, I'll be swigger-jiggered." He scratched his head.

"Go on, give it to her." Violet pointed to the lady with the baby.

Walter hesitated. He wasn't used to sharing good fortune.

"You can do it. It won't hurt you," I told him. "Might even make you feel good."

Walter's hand was wigglier than a loose tooth when he handed the lady the money.

She threw her arms around his neck and he turned stiff as a board.

"OK, OK. Enough of your carryin' on." Walter blushed.

Before she left, the lady got his address so she could pay him back. Then after he bought his own things with his credit card, Walter told us to follow him outside.

"I got somethin' for ya," he mumbled.

Noah and Leroy waited by the van. At the sight of Walter, my dog growled.

"Easy boy." Noah tugged on the rope leash.

Then Leroy spotted Walter's fanny pack. His shiny nose began to twitch as if inside there might be a great smelly treasure.

"What are you after, dog?" Walter looked puzzled and unzipped his pouch. To his amazement, he pulled out a crumpled bag that had

"For Your Favorite Pooch" printed on it. Inside, he found a piece of fatty steak. Leroy's favorite.

"Well, I'll be," said Walter, who was finally beginning to understand the power of his magical fanny pack.

Leroy licked Walter's hand and then snatched the meat.

"Hard as it is for me to say so, savin' somebody's life is probably more important than rackin' up a few more dang lottery tickets."

He opened the van door, pulled out Rosalie Claire's fanny pack, and handed it to me. "All charged up, good as new."

I thanked him and unzipped it. Inside was the honey-yellow nugget of frog amber.

"What about this?" I asked, holding it up.

"You might need it again for your granny. Though I'm guessin' you were twistin' the truth when you said it was Florida. Not a ghost of a chance that could be true."

I shrugged and said nothing. It was better if he believed that. Walter was only just learning about magic. He wasn't nearly ready to understand the wonders of time travel.

"Anyway, I shouldn't be needin' that amber for another thirty years. As long as I don't slip up and get too selfish, that is."

I had the urge to hug him, greasy overalls and all, but I stopped myself so he wouldn't get embarrassed.

"I'll tell you what. I'll leave the amber with Grandma Daisy. Then if you ever make a mistake, she could still recharge it overnight."

"I'd be much obliged, 'cuz Lord knows I'm not perfect."

"Who is?" I said. "Oh, and Walter? I have something for you, too."

I dug the newspaper clipping from my jeans pocket. "The ring was for Betty Montoya, wasn't it?"

Walter's eyes opened wide. "How in tarnation did you know that?"

"A good guess," I said and gave Walter the article. He studied it and looked so sad I thought he might cry.

"Betty and me, we'd been plannin' to marry, then she got cold feet. Gave me back the ring and took off. Who can blame her? I guess I wasn't always the nicest guy. But the thing is, I was a better man when she was around."

I was just about to zip up Rosalie Claire's fanny pack when I noticed something else inside. An envelope addressed to Walter, postmarked today. Weird.

"Looks like you got mail." I handed it over.

Walter opened it and pulled out a piece of pale pink stationery.

"It's from Betty. Glory be, I think this old blind squirrel just found himself an acorn."

Walter looked faint and sank onto the passenger seat of his van. The letter fluttered from his grasp and landed on the sidewalk. Violet snatched it and offered it back.

"Go ahead. You read it. Then tell me the devil's not playin' tricks on me."

She read it aloud.

Dear Walter,
I've been thinking about you every day for fifteen years. I'm sorry I left you like I did. I made a mistake. Or at least I think I did. I now live in Philadelphia, and I would like to be in touch and know how you're doing.
Please write back.

Your friend,
Betty Montoya

"Sweet niblets," gasped Violet.

"How in the world did that thing show up in your pouch?" Walter shook his head in disbelief.

"It was something you needed. After a while, you just learn to trust the magic," I said.

"This is the kind of magic a fella could get used to."

I swear it looked as if Walter's eyes were sparkling with a bajillion stars of happiness.

"And Walter?" said Violet. "If you're going to get Betty to like you again, you'd better think about getting yourself cleaned up."

I think he heard her, although it was hard to tell for sure. Walter appeared to be off in some other world, hypnotized by Cupid's arrow.

We said goodbye and wished him luck.

I had no idea if finding true love would wind up changing Walter's surly nature. I sure hoped so. But as my mom used to say, life doesn't come with a guarantee.

"I guess that means it's time to go back to Costa Rica and help your grandma," said Noah. "Besides, you owe me a surfing lesson."

I knew it was time to go, although I'd made a promise to my mom I wouldn't break.

In the distance we heard the honking of car horns and the clanging of cymbals. The parade was about to begin and my mom would be looking for us in the crowd. We had to hurry.

CHAPTER THIRTY-SIX
The Fiesta Parade

We wove our way along the crowded sidewalk, searching for a place to watch the parade. Finally, we squeezed into an open spot on the curb, a few doors up from the Wildflower.

The high school band led the pack, followed by a string of horses. Mostly the riders were dressed like circus clowns, except for a few who wore their everyday cowboy gear. Leroy hadn't seen that many horses in his life. He sniffed the air and panted with excitement.

Then came a hodgepodge of tractors, bulldozers, and pick-up trucks decorated with banners advertising practically everyone's business in town.

"Hey, Madison! Isn't that your neighbor who sold you Leroy?" Violet pointed to a black pick-up rolling our way, hauling a mountain of old computer parts. Duct-taped to the side of the truck, a sign said: *Manny's Computer Repair. Opening Soon!*

"That's him all right. And I bet I know where he's taking all that junk. Right to his backyard."

When the truck pulled alongside us, Manny waved in our general direction, and the parade came to a temporary stop.

That's when Leroy noticed who was driving. He trotted over to the front truck tire and lifted his leg.

Violet giggled. "Looks like Leroy recognizes him too."

"Talk about raining on the guy's parade," Noah said and the three of us laughed ourselves silly.

Even though the parade began to move again, Manny stayed put so he could shout a few curse words at Leroy for peeing on his tire. Then he revved his engine and took off to catch up with the pack of bulldozers and tractors.

The procession went on and on. Native American drummers beat out a rhythm on their buckskin drums. Miss Fiesta, wearing a tiara and a poofy lavender gown, rode in the back of a convertible, showing off her royal wave. Next, Smokey the Bear lumbered by, walking two poodles dressed like circus dogs. I felt sorry for the guy in that Smokey costume with the blistering sun blazing as hot as any forest fire.

"I hope your mom comes soon," Violet groaned. "I'm starving. And roasting."

"Seriously. I think it's hot enough to cook pancakes on my head," I said.

"You do that and I'll eat them," Violet joked.

That's when we heard the eruption of hoots and hollers from the crowd. Everyone pointed at a red and white circus tent on the back of a flatbed truck that was rolling our way. Grandpa Jack sat behind the wheel, his tape deck cranked up high, blasting the cheery sounds of circus music.

Leroy wagged his tail and barked. Attached to the back of the truck was the giant papier-mâché elephant on wheels we'd passed by the first time Mike drove us out to Walter's. Riding on top was Florida in all her glory. Her fire engine red sequined costume shimmered in the sun as she wriggled to the rhythm of the music, blowing kisses to the crowd. *Hang on, Florida,* I thought. *I'm coming back soon to Costa Rica to save your future self.*

I scanned the back of the float and recognized Florida's three best friends in their matching sequined suits, and just like my grandmother, they looked a whole lot younger. They held lacy umbrellas and pretended to walk back and forth on an invisible tightrope.

But where was my mom? Did Florida ground her? Or did she get cold feet?

I made my way into the street to get a better look. The four daughters of the Red Hot Mamas sat on the far side of the float, all in matching sparkly baby pink. Three of them hid their faces in embarrassment, but the girl on the end kept turning her head as if she was looking for someone.

It was my mom. Over her costume she wore cutoffs. It looked like Florida hadn't made her carry the Chicky Boom-Boom sign after all. When her eyes found me they softened, and she smiled. It was exactly the way she used to smile whenever I'd shown her a picture I'd drawn, or I'd given her a rose I'd just picked from our garden. She blew me a kiss, and Grandpa Jack rolled on down the street.

It was almost time to go back to the future. Even though the parade wasn't done, I was done with the parade. I'd kept my promise to my mom, and now I needed to say goodbye to Grandma Daisy. We walked a few doors down to the Wildflower.

"I can't wait to get back to Costa Rica, jump in the ocean, and *surf*," Violet said.

"Mind if I take my turn first?" Noah asked.

"Oh my gosh, I was a total surfboard hog, wasn't I? I'm so sorry." Violet's apology made Noah smile.

"Sometimes she gets a little excited," I said, and shrugged.

I pushed open the front door and took a deep breath. It wasn't going to be easy to say goodbye.

The Wildflower bustled with tourists. Grandma Daisy stood on her tiptoes, returning a stack of books to a shelf in the middle of the store, while Mike worked the cash register.

We told Grandma Daisy all about Walter, how he learned to use magic to help others, and that at last he'd returned Rosalie Claire's fanny pack.

Then I handed her the piece of magic amber. "Walter said he'll leave his pack with you overnight if it ever needs a recharge."

"You kids accomplished a miracle getting this back." Then Grandma Daisy looked at us and sighed. "I guess this means you're leaving."

We all nodded.

"Oh dear. I suppose that's the way of things." She took my hands in hers. "Best of luck with Florida. I hope she gets better."

"Thanks. Me too."

"And Madison? Someday when Angela finally knows she's your mom, she's going to be so proud of you. I can feel it in my bones."

I threw my arms around her and we hugged goodbye. I told her that I'd never forget her in a zillion years. When I noticed Violet and Noah standing awkwardly off to the side, looking a little left out, I motioned them over.

"Come on guys, group hug." The four of us pulled in close and draped our arms around each other.

Leroy whined.

"You too, boy," I said. "Get in here." He wriggled between our legs into the middle of our circle.

When we pulled apart, Mike looked up from the cash register.

"Bye kids. Hope to catch you in the future." And then he winked.

I made a note to myself that the next time I saw Future Mike, I'd ask him if this Mike was his dad.

By the time we went back outside, the parade had ended. A stream of spectators clogged the streets and sidewalks, shuffling toward Ralph Edwards Park.

There was one more person I needed to find so I could say goodbye.

That's when we heard an earsplitting explosion coming from down the street.

KA-BANG!

Leroy took off faster than a jackrabbit, yanking the rope leash from my hand. He disappeared into the crowd.

"Leroy!" I yelled. "Leroy, come!"

But Leroy was nowhere to be seen.

CHAPTER THIRTY-SEVEN
Chasing Down Leroy

"Sweet Mother Pickles, what was that?" Violet had plugged her ears with her fingers.

"Probably a whopper of a cherry bomb," Noah said. "Loud and harmless."

Unfortunately, Leroy didn't know that. The blast had sent him running for his life. As we raced through the crowd, we called out for him. We whistled. We asked everyone we passed if they'd seen a chubby wiry white dog on the loose. A few of them pointed in the direction of the park.

Ralph Edwards Park swarmed with people milling around the food booths and carnival games. A country western band blasted music with their amps on high.

Violet and I shouted for Leroy, and Noah let out a piercing two-fingered whistle. Even if he was close by, I wasn't sure he'd be able to hear us over the rowdy racket of the Fiesta.

First we checked the food booths since there's nothing my dog likes more than finding some little kid's dropped hot dog. No luck.

"If I were him, I'd get away from all this insanity," Noah said. "Should we check by the river?"

Of course! Leroy loved dunking himself in the Rio Grande and chasing mallard ducks he could never catch.

And that's exactly where we found him. Snuggled beside a blond-haired teenaged boy sitting on the riverbank.

"Your dog?" he asked.

I nodded and looked Leroy straight in the eye. "No more running off, boy. You scared me!" The instant he saw me he grinned, wagged his tail, and pierced the air with a few sharp barks. Then he gave the boy a sloppy lick on his cheek.

"I think he likes me." He grinned and wiped away the slobber.

Leroy plopped his head on the boy's lap.

"Those dudes were about to set off another cherry bomb. I told them it was flipping out the dog and to knock it off." He stroked Leroy's fuzzy head.

"Thanks," I said. I couldn't quite place it, although the boy looked like someone I knew.

Just then I heard a familiar voice.

"Well, look who's here!" It was my mom. She'd pulled her Bart Simpson t-shirt over her costume and she carried her video camera.

"I knew Leroy had good taste." She smiled, looking straight into the guy's bright blue eyes.

Was my mom flirting with him?

Leroy's new best friend smiled back at my mother.

Yep. Definitely flirting.

"I see you've met Danny."

His name was *Danny*?

"We haven't been officially introduced," he said.

My mom made the introductions. "Madison, Violet, Noah? This is my friend Danny McGee."

My skin tingled and every inch of my body buzzed. *It was my dad!* I thought my mom hadn't met him until college. But when I finally looked into his eyes, I had no doubt that he was my father. They were the same sky blue, exactly like mine. It was almost as if I was looking into a mirror.

Leroy panted, barked, and let out a long squeaky whine. I think maybe he knew it was my dad too. My mom used to say that things happen for a reason. Maybe this was the reason Leroy hitchhiked with us to the past. It was so he could lead me to my father.

Violet elbowed me in the side. She and Noah looked just as shocked as I did.

A zillion and one questions flooded my brain, although there was no way I could ask my kid-dad a single one of them. He wouldn't be able to answer. None of the stuff I wanted to know had happened yet.

"Hey, I'm going to go shoot some video," my mom said. "Who wants to come?"

"I do." My kid-dad scrambled to his feet.

"What about you guys?" she asked the rest of us.

Violet, Noah, and I traded looks.

Just as I'd promised, I'd watched my mom in the parade. Now I knew it was time to leave. This was truly goodbye.

"We have to go home," I said, and did my best not to cry. "I really wish I could stay."

My mom let out a sigh. "That's a drag. We'll see each other again, right?"

Eight years from now she would become my mom and see me on the morning I was born. Then we'd be together every day for the next ten years, nine months, and twenty-four days. But my time with her was done. Except of course in my heart and my memory, where she would live until I turned at least 103.

"Yeah, of course," I reassured her.

I threw my arms around my kid-mom and hugged her tight, breathing in her scent. It wasn't anything like her grown-up aroma of cinnamon and butterscotch. It was the fragrance of fresh vanilla and warm spun cotton candy.

"Thanks for everything. You're the best," she whispered in my ear.

"You too. I'll never forget you."

"Better not." My mom smiled. "Besides, you can't. We have these." She held up her moonstone bracelet that was just like mine. It sparkled in the sun.

She smiled at me warm and wide. I looked one last time into her eyes, soft brown flecked with gold. Then she turned with my future dad to walk toward the carnival games. I could just make out their conversation.

"Someday I'm leaving this place," she told him. "I'm thinking about going to college in San Francisco."

"That'd be cool," he said. "Maybe I'll come with you."

My dad took my mom's hand in his and they disappeared into the Fiesta crowd.

Leroy followed my friends and me downriver until we found a private place with no one around except for a red-winged blackbird spying on us from a willow tree.

I pulled the remote control from my backpack. Noah took Leroy by the collar and the three of us held hands. I took one last look around, and then I pressed the buttons.

PING!

CHAPTER THIRTY-EIGHT
Back to Costa Rica

The sticky night air of Costa Rica greeted us the instant we popped back into the lobby of La Posada Encantada. So did Grandpa Jack. He stared at us in a wide-eyed stupor. I flew straight into his arms.

"Sunshine! I've been waiting for you!"

"When did you get here?" I asked.

"'Bout twenty minutes ago, but I came the old fashioned way. On a plane and a taxi—not a crazy contraption like that. I'm glad Rosalie Claire put me in charge of keepin' an eye on the TV while she checked on Florida. It was a heck of a thing watchin' you pop outta there. Better than any show on TV."

Leroy nudged Grandpa until he reached down and scratched his fuzzy ears. Grandpa Jack said hello to Violet, who he'd met a year and a half ago at my mom's funeral. He stared for a split second at Noah as if he knew him, and then he shrugged.

"I don't believe we've met, son." He shook Noah's hand.

I wondered if there was ever a time that Grandpa Jack had remembered seeing us in his living room twenty years ago. If he had, it appeared that the memory had faded into thin air.

Grandpa told us that Rosalie Claire had called him before we'd left for the Amazon when Florida had taken a turn for the worse. He'd flown here as quickly as he could.

"It was bad enough she up and left Truth or Consequences without a word. I swear your grandmother is gonna be the death of me." He sighed and shook his head.

"Where is she?" I asked.

"With Rosalie Claire, back in the little yellow house. That fine woman is a livin', breathin' saint. She'll be pleased as a pumpkin to see you. Let's hope that fanny pack is working. Otherwise, Rosalie Claire's gettin' ready to send your grandma to the hospital."

No way did I want Florida going to a hospital. The magic *had* to work.

I grabbed the fanny pack from my backpack and we all hurried to the bungalow.

My grandmother slept beneath a paper-thin sheet, sweaty with a burning fever. She flailed from side-to-side, probably thrashing away bad dreams.

"Praise be, you're back and not a moment too soon!" Rosalie Claire stood up on her crutches and gave me a bear-sized hug. I gave her the fanny pack and she clipped it around her waist, took a deep breath, and slid open the zipper.

When she peered inside, a huge smile spread across her face.

"Hallelujah!" she cried.

The magic was back!

She pulled out a half-dozen glass dropper bottles filled with herbal potions. Each had a tiny typed label with instructions. She uncapped one and sniffed. Her face screwed up in disgust.

"I'm going to need a cup of warm water and lots of honey or I'll never get Florida to drink this."

I raced to the kitchen and returned with the water, honey, and a spoon.

Rosalie Claire added drops of the murky brown potions to the warm water, naming them one-by-one. Katuki, nibima, sweet wormwood, clove, and Ghana quinine. Then she poured in inky black goop from a sixth mysterious vial with no label. The only instruction was to use every single drop.

The bitter smell of the dark liquids swirling together tingled my nostrils and I plugged my nose.

Before stirring the tea, Rosalie Claire dumped in scads of honey. Then she woke up Florida, who was only half-conscious.

"Poison. You're poisoning me," my grandmother moaned as Rosalie Claire forced her to sip the foul potion.

"Drink it up, cupcake. It'll make you feel better." Grandpa Jack took Florida's hand.

Violet, Noah, and I watched my grandmother swallow the remedy until every last drop was gone.

"Now what?" Noah asked.

"Now we wait." Rosalie Claire crossed her fingers.

My friends and I looked at each other and we didn't have to say a word. We all crossed our fingers, too.

Grandpa Jack offered to sit by Florida's side, and Rosalie Claire took him up on it.

"Now that my pack is working again, it's high time I go treat this swollen ankle of mine."

She hobbled out of the room on her bamboo crutches, followed by Violet and Noah, but I stayed behind with my grandparents.

"Grandpa Jack, she's going to be OK, right?"

"I sure hope so, sweetie. You and I know better than anybody what a tough old bird your grandma can be. I'm thinkin' maybe that toughness will work in her favor."

Even though I was twelve, I climbed into Grandpa's lap and leaned my head against his whiskery cheek.

"I love you, Grandpa."

"I love you too, Sunshine."

We snuggled for a long time until Grandpa insisted that I go hang out with my friends. Leroy followed me to the lobby where they were waiting with Rosalie Claire. As she pulled out healing salves from her fanny pack and rubbed them on her ankle, we took turns telling her everything that had happened in Truth or Consequences, twenty years in the past.

CHAPTER THIRTY-NINE
Miracle Movers

Rosalie Claire must have asked at least a million-and-one questions about Grandma Daisy, Mike, my mom, and my dad before Noah noticed the MegaPix was still on. Grandma Daisy's tape had come to an end.

"Might as well switch it off. I think we're done with it for now," I said.

"We could decide to use the MegaPix to go somewhere else tomorrow." Violet's eyes fired up with mischief. "How about *America's Got Talent*? We could use the remote control to perform a disappearing act."

We all cracked up. Then Noah reminded her that tomorrow he was going surfing, and that's exactly what I wanted to do, too.

I hit the off button on the VCR and the TV switched to a nature channel. I picked up the remote, but before I could turn off the MegaPix, lightning waves crackled across the screen.

Leroy growled.

Out of the MegaPix popped a sweaty guy in khaki pants, a muddy t-shirt, and a Yankees cap. He clutched a filthy remote control, caked in stinky brown goo.

"Where in the blazes am I now? This isn't my living room. Please tell me I'm not on another blasted TV show!"

He turned around and looked at the MegaPix in horror. A lion snarled at the screen. The man pointed his remote at the TV and hit off.

I heard the click of the side lobby door and shuffling footsteps. For the first time since he'd checked in at the hotel, I saw the wrinkly old man with thinning gray hair. The travel writer from Room Three.

"No Donald, you're not on another TV show," he said. "Sorry, you got stuck. It was taking you so long that for the first time ever, I had to put your show on repeat so you could come back out. It must have played over and over for weeks. Finally, I just couldn't wait. We had a state of emergency here and I needed to pick up the MegaPix."

Then the old man turned to me. "Hello, Squirt," he said. And he winked.

"Mike?!" I shot a look at Violet and Noah. They seemed as confused as me.

"Well, of course it's you, Mike," said Rosalie Claire. "I should have known that."

"Wait, you're not the guy who delivered my MegaPix." The man took off his Yankees cap and scratched his balding head.

"I am one and the same," admitted Mike.

How could he suddenly be so *old*? "Are you the same Mike we just saw in 1994 who worked at the Wildflower, or was that your dad?" I asked.

"Definitely not my dad. That would have been me, Squirt."

"How is that even possible?" Noah asked.

From under his shirt Mike pulled out a thick gold chain. Dangling on it was a lumpy silver coin, etched with ancient words in a foreign alphabet. "It's a magic Celtic amulet I came across in an antique store in France. This little baby lets me shape shift from an old man to a young one and back again. Makes it a lot easier to lift heavy objects when you're a young guy. Gives me a little more energy, too."

I asked him how old he *really* was, with no shape shifting involved.

"Eighty," he said. "Although I don't think I look a day over seventy-nine." Then he broke into a huge grin.

"Holy guacamole." Violet looked as if she might faint.

"This is the most awesome thing yet," Noah said. "So doing the math, it means in 1994 when you looked twenty, you were really *sixty*?"

"What can I say? It's a gift." Mike shrugged. "And the truth is, no matter how old I look or how old I am, on the inside I still feel as young as a teenager."

When I really looked at eighty-year-old Mike, I could see he was exactly the same person, down to his wink and his smile. He was just a whole lot older.

"Excuse me," said Donald. "I hate to interrupt the party, but does anyone have any idea how I'm going to get back home to New York City?"

"I can give you a lift," Mike offered. "My rig's parked a few blocks away. Hold your horses and I'll be right back."

He tottered out the front door. It wasn't long before we heard the Miracle Movers delivery truck pull up.

Violet, Noah, and I rushed outside to watch the door swing open. The familiar version of Mike hopped out. He was young with a scruffy red beard.

"Ta-da! Same old me. Or should I say 'same young me?' Kind of nice to have collected eighty years' worth of wisdom and still have the muscle power to move a MegaPix."

A year ago, before I'd known anything about magic, none of this would have made any sense. But now, not much surprised me. Even the fact that Mike had switched from a young guy to an old one, and back again.

When Donald saw Mike he did a double take. "*Now* you look like the delivery guy. This switcho-chango business may even be stranger than teleporting into a TV." He held up the smelly remote control. "Why don't you take this thing before anything else happens?"

He handed it to Mike who scrunched up his nose. Rosalie Claire propped herself up on her crutches, pulled a Ziploc bag from her fanny pack, and gave it to Mike. He dropped in the remote so the truck wouldn't stink of lion poop. Then Violet, Noah, and I helped load the MegaPix into the truck.

"Well, I suppose my Costa Rican vacation is officially over." Mike looked a little sad when he said it.

"I guess you weren't writing a book on travel after all?" I asked.

Mike grinned. "Sure I was, Squirt. *Time* travel." And we all cracked up.

There was one last thing that still gnawed at me. "Mike? How did you know to come here?"

He shrugged. "Call it a hunch. I had a feeling you might be in need of a guardian angel. Someone to look after you, just in case. Of course it didn't hurt that once I was here, I overheard you kids through the wall of my hotel room, talking about wanting the MegaPix back." Then he winked.

Now I knew I'd recognize that wink anywhere, anytime.

After we said our goodbyes, Mike and Donald climbed into the Miracle Movers truck. We watched it rattle down the bumpy road. Even in the night's darkness we could see it shimmer like heat waves bouncing off the pavement. Then it faded and disappeared, bound for New York City.

CHAPTER FORTY
The Miracles of Magic

The next morning, I woke up early with the sun. I'm pretty sure I'd kept my fingers crossed the whole night, hoping the potion had worked its magic on Florida. Violet, Noah, and Leroy were still asleep. As I listened to the waves breaking on the shore, I tried my best to picture my kid-mom and my kid-dad. I dug under the bed for my sketchbook and pencils and drew the two of them holding hands in a field of sunflowers under a rainbow arching in the sky. It was exactly how I wanted to remember my parents.

When Noah woke up, he had surfing on the brain.

"Is it time to go to the beach? Last night Thomas promised he'd teach me to hang ten." He dug a clean swimsuit out of his suitcase.

Violet peeked out from under the covers. "Not until we eat something. The whole night I dreamed of chili dogs and cotton candy. Do you realize we were at a fair and didn't eat a single bite of junk food? I feel deprived."

"Not me. I feel *relieved*," said Noah. "That stuff is gross. Bad for your body. Scientific fact."

"This is no time to be a brainiac, Noah. I. Need. Food."

While Noah slipped into the bathroom to change into his swimsuit, Violet and I pulled on ours. Then we put on our t-shirts and flip-flops, and headed to breakfast at Thomas's Café. My growly stomach told me I was just as hungry as Violet.

"If it isn't the return of the time-traveling heroes." Thomas gave us a two-fingered salute.

"Have you seen Florida this morning? Is she any better?" I hoped and prayed he'd say yes.

"She slept quietly through the night for the first time since she's been here, if that tells you anything. Still sawing logs, I think."

I took that as a good sign.

We picked our favorite table under the shade of the palm grove, and Thomas handed out menus. "Eat up. We have a big day ahead of us. Breakfast is on the house."

"Thanks, Thomas! But breakfast is always on the house," I reminded him.

"So it is. Well then, you better order double." That made Violet happy even though there wasn't much in the way of junk food on the menu.

Thomas disappeared into the kitchen to whip up our breakfast.

We stuffed ourselves silly. Even Leroy got his own plate of bacon and eggs. Violet and Noah were anxious to hit the beach, but first I needed to stop by the bungalow.

We pushed open the front door. The first thing we noticed? Grandma Daisy's old trunk.

"How cool is it that just yesterday we saw that thing twenty years ago? My mind is now officially bent." Violet smacked her forehead, trying to make sense of the whole thing.

Without warning, a familiar funny feeling swirled inside me. I kneeled down, unlatched the trunk, and pushed open the lid. For some reason, I wasn't at all surprised that on top was something that hadn't been there the last time we'd looked. A white envelope addressed to me. Underneath was a sandy brown fanny pack with a daisy stamped on it. The one that had belonged to Grandma Daisy.

"No way! Awesome!" Violet's mouth gaped open wide.

"*So* awesome!" Noah agreed.

I tore open the envelope and read the note inside.

Dear Madison:

I hope my fanny pack finds its way to you because I know you'll use it wisely. Taking on someone else's pack can be tricky. I'm sure eventually you'll teach it to behave!

Love, Grandma Daisy

"OK, that is *so* freaky," said Violet.

"Grandma Daisy is the coolest." I clipped my new fanny pack around my waist. It fit perfectly. When I pulled open the zipper and peered inside, I could barely breathe. Glowing like golden honey was the magical nugget of frog amber. I couldn't wait to tell Rosalie Claire.

Just as I was about to close the trunk, I noticed something else I hadn't seen before. A newspaper clipping, yellowed with age. I pulled it out and read.

"Oh my goodness!" gasped Violet, who peered over my shoulder.

It was a wedding announcement from 1996. Walter and Betty had gotten married in Philadelphia, where they'd opened a tire shop. In the photo they glowed with happiness.

"He cleaned himself up, just like I told him," said Violet.

Walter was smiling wide, looking handsome in a suit and tie. Peeking out from his jacket was his fanny pack. I slid the article back into the trunk.

"So with Walter getting married, we might have changed the future a little bit after all," Noah said.

"But in the best way," I pointed out, and we all high-fived.

"What's all the ruckus?" Grandpa Jack poked his head out of the bedroom. "Don't be strangers, come on in."

Florida was still sound asleep. Rosalie Claire sat by her bedside.

"Well look what you have on," she said when she noticed my new fanny pack. "I've always wondered what Grandma Daisy did with that.

It must have been waiting for the right time to show up for just the right person." She beamed ear-to-ear.

My grin matched hers, times ten.

"How's Florida?" I asked.

"I think she's finally on the road to recovery." Rosalie Claire exhaled a giant sigh of relief. "I stayed up all night, keeping an eye on her. I don't think we need to worry about calling the hospital in San José."

Suddenly, I felt the weight of all my hospital fears flying fast and far away.

Florida stirred and peeked open an eye. "Oh my word, I had the most alarming dreams. Giant tarantulas, dinosaurs, little blue aliens."

"Are you feeling better?" I asked. "I've been worried about you."

"Thanks, honey. I do believe I'm on the mend. Although I'm sure I must look like an utter train wreck."

"I might have something to help with that." My fingers trembled as I unzipped my new fanny pack and hoped to discover exactly what Florida needed. A hairbrush, lipstick, maybe a little blush? I peered inside and found . . . a rubber band ball.

I shrugged. "I guess my new fanny pack and I have a little work to do."

My friends cracked up.

"It always takes some time and training for them to get used to a new owner," Rosalie Claire said.

"If anyone can do it, it's you, Madison," Violet said. "After all, you trained Leroy, right?"

"Yep, I sure did," I said. And someday soon I'd train this magic pouch too.

I think the best thing of all was that Florida didn't seem to mind a bit that I hadn't found her any beauty products.

"Don't you worry. When I get back my old get-up-and-go, I'm sure I'll be ready for some all-important beautification. By the way, where did you get that charming little bracelet? I seem to recall your mother had one just like it."

I ran my finger along the moonstones surrounding my wrist. "She did," I said. "It's one of my favorite things."

"It's divine. It looks lovely on you." Florida closed her eyes and drifted off to a peaceful sleep. A slight smile curved up the corners of her mouth. Right then and there I knew that when my vacation was over, going home to Truth or Consequences with Florida and Grandpa Jack suited me just fine.

CHAPTER FORTY-ONE
Surf's Up!

"Ready to learn how to hang ten?" Thomas asked.

"Yes!" Noah raised his fist, eager to take on the challenge.

"Since Jack's with Florida, and my ankle is feeling much better, I'm tagging along," Rosalie Claire said. "Besides, someone needs to watch Leroy so he doesn't go plunging into the water after Madison."

I could always count on Rosalie Claire.

We trooped across the inn's grounds toward the beach, our surfboards tucked under our arms. Thomas had rented two extras so Violet and Noah could have their own. Rosalie Claire limped behind us without her crutches. Whatever she'd rubbed on her ankle had sped up her recovery lickety-split.

On the way we ran into Riptide and Wingnut. They were heading back after a morning of riding the waves.

"Dudes, I've been thinking about that GPS gizmo you hooked up to my laptop. Did you win the game?" Riptide asked.

Violet, Noah, and I looked at each other and smiled. "Sure did," I said. "We won it big time." In fact, meeting my kid-mom and my kid-dad, and saving my grandmother, felt as if I'd just won the million-dollar jackpot.

"Gnarly, dudes! Catch you later!" He and Wingnut shuffled back to the inn.

The second we made it to the beach, Leroy charged ahead of us, barreling straight for the sparkling Pacific Ocean.

"We can't let him hit the water before we do. Race you!" Violet shouted.

We dropped our boards on the shore and leaped into the salty sea, Violet, Noah, Rosalie Claire, Thomas, Leroy, and me. I don't think anything ever felt better in my whole life. The rippling water was warm and crystal clear. In a single splash I erased all of the dust of Truth or Consequences, New Mexico.

Leroy dog-paddled in circles around us, barking with happiness.

We bodysurfed until we were breathless and then took a break on the beach, watching the waves. Today they were perfect.

"I think it's time to hit it," Thomas said.

I headed over to my surfboard, but Leroy got there first. He plunked himself right in the middle, doing his best Statue of Liberty imitation.

"Here we go again. Leroy, time to get off," I said.

Leroy refused to budge. He thumped his tail and let out three sharp barks.

"You know what, Madison? Maybe that dog isn't trying to protect you at all," said Rosalie Claire. "I think he wants a surfing lesson."

Leroy grinned and barked again.

"Well, why didn't you say so, boy?" I asked.

"I think he did. We just didn't understand him until now." Rosalie Claire hobbled over and stroked his wet fur.

Thomas slid his board to the water's edge and pushed it into the shallows. "OK, big guy, you're riding with me. Hop on."

With a happy yelp, Leroy charged off my board and sailed right onto Thomas's.

We floated our surfboards into the water until we were waist deep. Then we slid onto our bellies and paddled beyond the whitewater. Leroy sat on Thomas's board, his tail splashing water every time he wagged.

Thomas was an amazing teacher. Noah only wiped out three times, and before he knew it, he managed to stand up for the whole ride in, right along with Violet. Leroy learned to sit on the front of a surfboard as if he'd been doing it ever since he was a young pup.

Thomas even gave me a few new tips that had me surfing without a single wobble. Rosalie Claire did her part, watching from the beach and cheering each time we made it all the way in.

When my legs got tired, I took a break and drifted on my board. I watched my friends as they worked hard to stay upright and ride the waves. I loved how they were both so determined to get it right. My best friend Violet, who was always so gutsy and ready for anything; and brainy determined Noah, who I was beginning to think understood the power of hunches, just like me.

I looked up at the white fluffy picture clouds floating overhead and spied a spouting whale, a dragon, and an angel with feathery wings. I thought of my mom and my dad and how lucky I was that the magic had finally brought us back together. And now I knew deep in my bones that the three of us would be connected, forever and always.

Just then a perfect turquoise wave rose up and curled behind me. I popped onto my feet and, like a firebird, I flew straight toward the shore.

ACKNOWLEDGMENTS

Heartfelt thanks to one and all who helped me along the way. To my husband Steve who never failed to put aside anything he was doing to read a new draft; to my son Jordan for his eagle eye and keen insights; to my incredible editor, K.L. Going, who kept me on track when I wandered off of it; to my agent at CineLit, Mary Alice Kier; and to David Skinner, who had a soft spot for Madison McGee from the beginning. And most of all, to my early young readers who were fans *of Hello There, We've Been Waiting for You!* and couldn't wait for the second book to find out what happened next – Evelyn Cantwell, Sophie Eldridge, Addison Kocurek, Sadie Miller, Sydney Vernon, and Sophie Vernon. My readers are the ones who truly provide the magic. I want you to know, I wrote this for you.

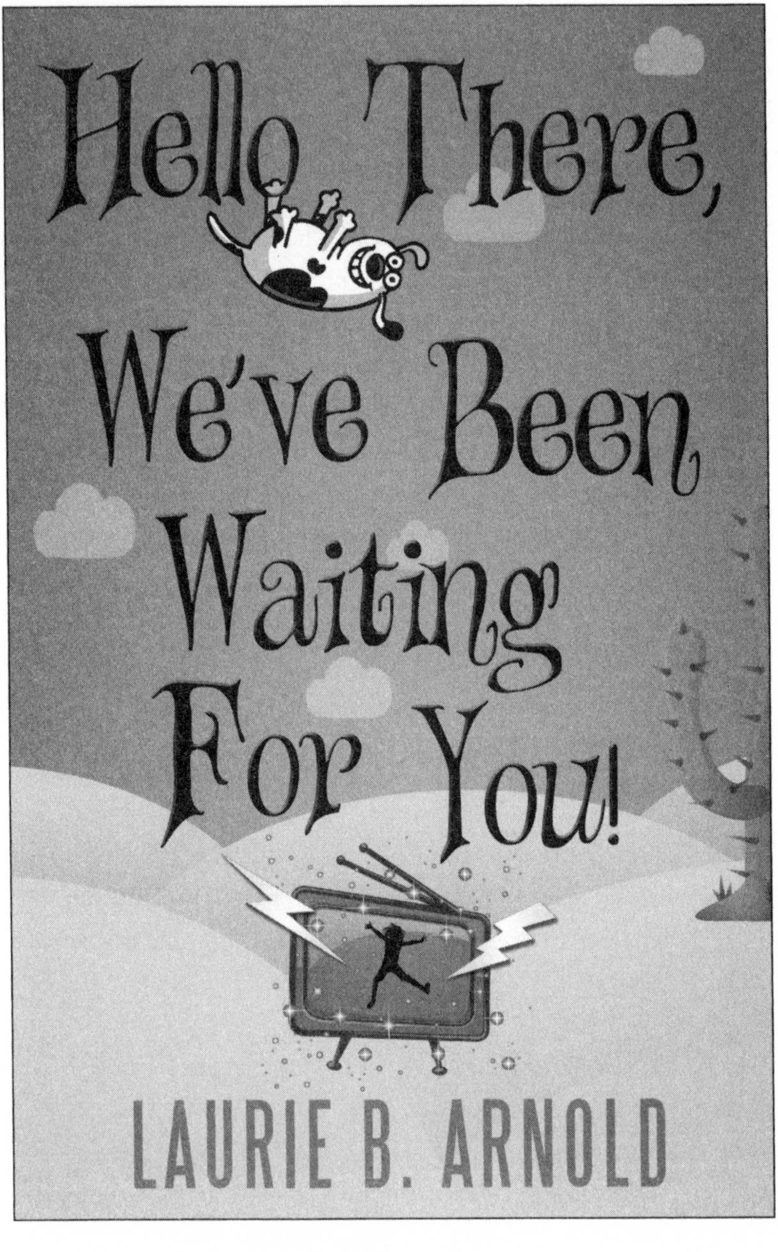
Hello There, We've Been Waiting For You!
LAURIE B. ARNOLD

You've read and loved *Hello There, Do You Still Know Me?*

In case you missed the first book in this series, check out
Hello There, We've Been Waiting For You!

"Author Arnold's debut novel, the first in a trilogy about Madison's adventures with the MegaPix, is fun and fantastical, with wacky characters that burst off the page and into readers' hearts. . . . A worthy romp that manages to teach powerful lessons as it entertains."
— *Kirkus Reviews*

When Madison McGee is orphaned and forced to live with her eccentric grandmother in boring old Truth or Consequences, New Mexico, she's pretty sure nothing will ever be right again. Her grandmother is addicted to TV shopping shows. Her only neighbors are a crazy lady and a vicious junkyard mutt. And she misses her old life something fierce. Could it get any worse?

Everything changes when a MegaPix 6000 TV mysteriously shows up on her doorstep. With the accidental push of a button on the remote control, Madison teleports into a dizzying world of lights, cameras, action, and peril. But with the help of a little magic, she discovers that things aren't always what they appear to be, and that life can actually get better in a brand new way.

Also published by Prospecta Press – www.prospectapress.com
$9.95 paperback and $5.99 eBook
Order from your favorite retailer or online at Indiebound.com,
Amazon.com, bn.com and Powells.com

About the Author

Laurie B. Arnold has two grown-up sons and lives in Bainbridge Island with her amazing husband and a perfect fuzzy dog. In addition to novels, she's written countless children's computer games, a trio of picture books, and scripts for animated kids' TV shows, including *Dragon Tales*.